Madeleine went into Durell's room and stood looking at his bed, as she had looked at many beds before. This started a quickening sensation within her that surprised her, because a man was nothing new to her, and what she planned to do was no novelty. Yet she realized it might be different with this one.

She loosened the catch on her skirt and let it rustle down her hips and thighs to the floor. She took off her blouse, shook her hair loose, and kicked away her shoes. There was nothing else to worry about—she wore no underwear.

She sat down naked on Durell's bed and waited for him.

Assignment . . . . .
Madeleine

EDWARD S. AARONS

A FAWCETT GOLD MEDAL BOOK

Fawcett Publications, Inc., Greenwich, Conn.
Member of American Book Publishers Council, Inc.

Chapter One

A COLD, August rain fell over Paris on the morning Durell arrived. He had flown from Washington to London, changing to an Air France plane at the London airport. He didn't think anyone had spotted him. McFee had arranged for a man to move promptly into Durell's apartment near Rock Creek Park in Washington, and the man looked enough like Durell to fool anyone who might be keeping him under surveillance back home. He was not sure about this, so he was careful as always. It was growing more difficult to develop and maintain a cover identity with each succeeding trip abroad.

From the airport in Orly he took a rattly taxi into Paris and checked in at the King George V Hotel, where a reservation had been made for him by Fred Hanson, out of the Embassy on the Place de la Concorde. The cold rain was quite a change after the humidity of Washington, but Durell did not mind it. Being in Paris, and having a chance to see Deirdre, was enough for the moment.

He telephoned her at once, before he shaved and bathed. She'd had no idea he was coming to Paris.

"Sam, darling, are you really here? You're not joking?"

"Here, in the flesh," he assured her. "Yearning, of course."

He listened to the soft throatiness of her laughter and reacted warmly to her delight. "No more than I, darling. Where are you?"

"Where I usually stay," he said.

"But I'm not sure—"

"I don't know about your telephone, Dee. Do you understand?"

5

Her voice fell. "Oh, Sam. You didn't come over to see me. For a crazy minute, I thought you'd taken some time off just to fly back with me. Can you do that?"

"No, I'm working. I'm sorry."

"Will it be for long?"

"I think so. Please, Dee. Not on the phone."

"But nobody is watching me! I'm just covering the fashion news, that's all! Who'd be interested in me, Sam?"

"You're my girl," he said. "That might be enough to do it."

Some of the joy went out of her voice. He heard her sigh, and he listened to the faint humming in the receiver at his ear. He was watchful for any telltale clicks that might indicate her line was bugged. He told himself he was probably being overly cautious, but there was no harm in that. Better to be too cautious than too dead. In Durell's business, the price of survival was constant suspicion and care, awake or asleep.

"Deirdre?"

"Yes, Sam. I'm so disappointed. I'm flying back to Washington tonight, didn't you know? I've been dreaming about you and me back home—making the most marvelous plans. But now you're here, and you'll be sleeping here in Paris, and I'll be over the Atlantic, with my dreams as empty as the sky and the sea. Sam, I can't stand it."

"I'm sorry," he said again. "You know how it is."

"Can I come to your room? Right now?"

"It isn't that I wouldn't want you. You know that, Dee. But make it Jacques' place. Know where it is?"

"Near the Salon Sofie."

"Right."

"If you say so. At one?"

"One," he said.

"Sam?"

"I love you," Durell said, and he hung up.

He bathed and shaved in the big, tessellated bathroom and changed into a dark blue suit, a white shirt with a soft button-down collar, and a solid maroon necktie. Durell was tall and long-legged, well muscled, in his thirties. He had thick dark hair, a small black moustache, and blue eyes that often turned dark when he was thoughtful or angry. He had deft, gambler's hands and the quick temperament of his Cajun parents combined with the instincts of a gambler, instilled in him by his

6

grandfather, who had worked the last of the old Mississippi side-wheelers.

He had started in the business with G-2 and later transferred to the old OSS training at Pemberley in England with the Jed teams during World War II. Afterward, he had known there could never be any other work for him, and he had been accepted by the Central Intelligence Agency of the State Department when it was first formed. Now he was sub-chief of K Section, under General Dickinson McFee. It was lonely, dangerous, mean and dirty work, and the risks went unheralded by bugles. Death walked with the man who yielded to a moment's carelessness, or who was unlucky, and death came in mean, small ways—in a Hong Kong alley, a train in Poland, a traffic accident on Fifth Avenue in Manhattan. It came with a knife, a garrote, or a push under crushing, spinning wheels. Durell knew that with the MVD at No. 2 Dzerzhinsky Square in Moscow there was a full dossier on him. He did not underestimate the enemy. He had already anticipated their knowledge of his presence here in Paris.

He lit a cigarette and looked down from the hotel window at the rain falling on the Avenue George V. Deirdre moved in him like a deep pang of loneliness. He watched a man and woman and two children hurrying along in the rain toward the hotel entrance, all laughter and love, and he knew he could never be a part of such a picture. Not for him the ordinary, everyday wonders of simple existence. In his business, the man who walked alone walked in safety. He had told Deirdre this often, but she had not yet accepted it.

He hadn't been in Paris since he had helped Orrie Boston get set up. Orrie was in Algeria now, moving in perilous waters to gather information on the Nationalist rebellion. His data would be sifted and collated and synthesized back in K Section, in Washington, and arranged for McFee's weekly conferences with Joint Chiefs, the Pentagon, State, and White House for future evaluations.

Orrin Boston had been father and mother to Durell during his training at the Maryland farm where Orrin was one of the chief instructors for the candidates aspiring to work for the CIA. Those hadn't been easy weeks, Durell recalled. You were tested for leadership and ingenuity in dozens of grueling ways. There were no rules of fair play at The Farm. Every dirty trick in the book was sprung on you. You trusted no one—not your fellow candidates, who would cajole you into friendship, nor the instructors, who could use a paternal attitude to suddenly trip you up and slide a knife across your throat. Durell enjoyed those weeks. Orrin Boston had been the oldest man at The Farm, pushing fifty, but he went through the obstacle courses with the toughest of them. A calm man with a lined face, carefully groomed gray hair, large and sensitive eyes, Orrin had a wife and three children in Chevy Chase, and he looked the suburban part. You would never suspect he was a spy and a skilled killer, a master of seven languages, with an intimate knowledge of the alleys and byways of dozens of the world's major cities.

Durell was in Paris now because of Orrie Boston. McFee had explained it simply.

"You know Orrie better than any of us, Sam. He belongs behind a desk in analytical work, but you know how short-handed we are and our troubles with the budget made us send him to Africa. He gets on very well with Paris Intelligence and the Deuxième Bureau—they know we have men in Algeria and they don't mind, as long as our services cooperate with their intelligence people. Orrie lived in Algiers as an export house manager, before the war, and he was one of our experts during the North African campaign. You knew him then, didn't you?"

Durell nodded. "We watched the 9th Infantry hit the beach at Ferruch. We were in a villa overlooking the shore. The place had been vacated by some members of the German Armistice Commission, and they left a lot of champagne, and Orrie and I were mighty thirsty after two months in the desert. We tied on a good one that night."

McFee permitted himself a brief smile. "Orrie speaks some of the Berber Kabyle dialects like a native. The Moslems trust him and the French trust him, so we had to use him over there. We've had some informative reports from Orrie, especially of those dealing with schisms among the Nationalist guerrillas. It's been useful in formulating State policy, though I sometimes wish they'd listen a little more to what Boston has had to say. But Orrie hasn't said much lately."

"Is he in trouble?" Durell asked.

8

"We don't know. We haven't heard from him."

Durell's face went blank. "For how long?"

"Two weeks."

"How much is he overdue?"

"Ten days." McFee sighed. "Georges Brumont suggests we send someone to look for him. Brumont is our liaison with the Deuxième Bureau. His own people have failed to get at the root of the trouble—I don't have any details—but there will be more for you in Paris when you get there. I don't like sending you abroad so soon, though, Sam. Our jokers will be on the lookout for you. I'd hate to lose you."

"I'll manage. When do you want me to go over?"

"As soon as you can pack. You know how I feel about Orrie. And I know how close you've been to him. If he's in trouble, help him out of it. If he's disappeared, find out where and why, and bring him back. If he's dead. . . ." McFee shuffled papers on his desk. He looked tired, a small man with the tremendous weight of life and death on his military shoulders. "You'll contact Brumont. He'll fill you in. Be careful—and tactful. You know how touchy the French are about Algeria."

Remembering McFee's words, Durell turned away from the rainy window of his Paris hotel room. He wished he could get rid of his nagging worry about Orrin Boston, but it wasn't easy. Your friends in the business were men you respected and admired. Clever, capable, brilliant men. But now and then somebody slipped, made a small error—and it was enough. The enemy was equally brilliant, deadly, and competent. And you lost a friend.

He hoped it wouldn't be that way with Orrie Boston.

The telephone rang in his room. He had been expecting Georges Brumont to call momentarily. He said, "Yes?" and Brumont's voice, in French, said, "We are happy you made a safe and swift voyage, m'sieu. We are anxious to confer on the business at hand. You were told in London of our meeting place?"

"Yes, I was," Durell said.

"Can you be there in half an hour?"

"Yes."

"Bon. I shall be waiting."

Durell hung up and shrugged into his raincoat. Then he went back to the window again, but he saw nothing of importance on the wide avenue in front of the hotel. He went out, locking the door automatically, but not concerned, because nothing in his luggage would be of interest to anyone who cared to look into it.

The Salon Sofie was on the Left Bank beyond the Pont-Neuf. A series of terraces overlooked the Seine and the bridges and parks, but in today's rain the chairs and tables were empty, and the manikins were working indoors. Durell paid off his taxi two blocks from the salon and walked along the river bank before climbing the stone steps to the street. Gray ribbons of rain wavered across the dimpled surface of the water. The trees wept in gray melancholia, and he could not see the Eiffel Tower because of the fog. Nobody followed him.

He looked at his watch as he passed Jacques' café, but he was an hour early to meet Deirdre, and the people under the striped awning, seated in the wrought-iron chairs at the round iron tables, all looked unfamiliar. He went on and pushed open the ornate glass and gold doors of the Salon Sofie.

Chapter Two

A woman with green hair dusted with silver greeted him, smiling politely, and ushered him through a carpeted, mirrored foyer into the main room. Two men, obviously American tourists, sat on a banquette in the foyer; they looked alternately worried about their wives' extravagances and then, when a model swayed by, forgot their worries while the girl was in view. Durell followed the woman with the green hair into the main salon. Neither American was interested in him.

"I am Madame Sofie," the woman said. "You are expected. Over there, please."

Durell saw Georges Brumont and Fred Hanson, from the Embassy, seated in gilt Louis XIV chairs in front of a tall mirror. One end of the room was curtained off as a stage, with a low ramp reaching down to a wide circle of oyster white carpeting. The manikins moved in stilted, stylized postures, displaying clothing and figures to half-a-dozen whispering women. Durell paused to watch a willowy blonde with unprecedented breasts posture in a negligee. The blonde looked at him and smiled.

"Madeleine will be out shortly," Madame Sofie said.

"She has been upset, naturally, but your friends have been very patient."

"Madeleine?"

"Mademoiselle Sardelle. Tell the gentlemen that I will try again to hurry her along." The enamel moved in a smile again. "You will excuse me now, m'sieu?"

"With reluctance," Durell said.

She looked surprised at his gallantry and her smile widened; then she moved off, the silver dust glistening in her green hair. Durell crossed the deep carpeting to join Brumont and Hanson.

Fred Hanson's handshake was strong and firm. He was a career man in the Foreign Service, with pale hair groomed in a brush cut that gave him an American collegiate stamp. His family was upper Westchester, his clothing was Brooks Brothers, and his Phi Beta Kappa key came from Yale.

"Hi, Sam, right on the dot. You know Georges?"

"We met last year," Durell said, shaking hands with Brumont.

"Quite a spot for a rendezvous, eh?" Hanson said. "Soft music, gorgeous girls, perfumed air—"

"Please be seated, M. Durell," Brumont said bluntly. "You know that we have bad news for you?"

"No, I didn't know."

"You were not advised in London?"

"I saw no one of importance in London. Is this place safe?"

"Madame Sofie works for us on occasion. An unusual woman, because she keeps a closed mouth. That is one reason we meet here. There is also the manikin, Mlle. Sardelle. You will see her soon."

"What's the bad news?" Durell asked.

"Orrin Boston is dead," Hanson said. He was watching the models on the ramp. "One of our own men killed him."

Durell's face did not change. None of the sick dismay welling up in him showed through his gambler's impassive expression. But it was difficult to imagine Orrie Boston as dead. He had told himself to expect it, to be ready for it and accept it, as he had accepted such news before. But this was harder to take. It was almost impossible. He didn't believe it yet.

Brumont said quietly, "He was a friend of yours, m'sieu?"

11

"A very good friend."

"It is the war we fight, of course. I am sorry."

"Was he careless?" Durell asked.

"He was betrayed, as Hanson suggests. By your own man."

"Who?"

"The Happy One," Brumont said.

Durell looked at the Deuxième Bureau expert. Brumont was short, dark, and stout, with a thick moustache and heavy jowls. His hands were small and pale, the nails neatly manicured. He wore the Continental dark herringbone suit with wide, pointed lapels, the usual crushed black felt hat, a striped silk shirt, and a loosely knotted dark tie. His eyes were like small dark stones, examining Durell.

"The murderer's name is Charles L'Heureux," Brumont said. "An American of Canadian extraction, I believe. Do you know him?"

"No. Where is he now?"

"In military custody in the town of Marbruk, where the FLN, the Algerian rebels, staged their massacre some time ago. You know of the crime?"

"I read about it," Durell said. He looked at Hanson. "When and why did Orrin accept Charley L'Heureux to work with him?"

Hanson still watched one of the models moving on the ramp. He looked like a college boy in a burlesque house. "L'Heureux worked in Algeria for the past month. I don't know if you ever heard of him. He wasn't assigned to your section."

"No, he wasn't," Durell said.

"Well, anyway, he was one of our ex-G.I.'s—he's a French Canadian from Maine, by the way—who stayed over here after the war. No youngster now, of course. We have a file on him over at the Embassy—not a very shining record, you see, but a useful man in your sort of business." There was a curl of condescension in Hanson's voice. "L'Heureux is smart, lots of guts, supposed to have been in the old black-market rackets working the Mediterranean area after the war. But he was never caught or convicted at anything. Knows North Africa like the palm of my hand—which I'd like to use on that babe over there. The brunette, I mean."

"You son of a bitch," Durell said. His voice was thin. "You just said Boston is dead and—"

12

Hanson's eyes moved in shock and surprise. "He is."

"Then get your thoughts out from between your legs and let's hear more about it."

"Now, wait, you needn't get sore because I don't weep tears about Orrin Boston—"

"Please, gentlemen," Brumont said.

"All right." Durell sat back, the anger in him sinking to a controllable level. "Let's hear about L'Heureux and Orrin."

"You people hire characters like Charley L'Heureux, but he'd never be accepted for the Foreign Service, I assure you," Hanson said stiffly. "A black-marketeer, an adventurer, a man suspected by Brumont's people of more than one murder, a man with an Arab wife—maybe several of them—what do you expect, using him in a sensitive spot like Algeria?"

"How long was he on the payroll?"

Hanson shrugged. "A year or more, so far as we know. He was located here in Paris until recently, and then Orrin sent word up, asking specifically for L'Heureux. Boston said he was working as an intermediary, contacting the Moslems and dissident groups within the FLN, and he needed L'Heureux' help. He also implied there was something sour about L'Heureux and he wanted to keep an eye on him, and the best way to do that was to have L'Heureux assigned to him. So it was done, and who's to blame for what happened?"

"What did happen, exactly?"

"Apparently L'Heureux never got over his old habits. He was running guns to various Nationalist factions as a sideline to his work for you people. A rotten apple in the barrel, all right. Orrin must have gotten a line on the activities L'Heureux was directing from up here and had him sent down to pin the mark on him once and for all. But L'Heureux was smarter and quicker. All we've got is the wire from Marbruk, from the French commandant there. L'Heureux and Orrin had a fight and Orrin was killed. L'Heureux was captured trying to get through to rebel guerrilla lines and he's in solitary confinement at this moment."

"Why hasn't he been brought here?"

Brumont said quietly, "It is a delicate situation. Such an order was given, in truth. Naturally, the French authorities wished to take part in this, but after consultation with your Embassy, we felt it might be best to let

13

you wash your linen in private, as you say. We will waive all extradition rights to L'Heureux. He is all yours."

"But he's still in Marbruk?"

Brumont nodded. "There has been some serious fighting in that area. The telegraph lines are down, the radio from Tunis is jammed, and we get only garbled messages from the military post where it happened. At the moment, no one can be spared to escort L'Heureux back from the frontier. Unless you wish to wait a few days for the situation to clarify itself, you will have to go and get him yourself. You can do whatever you wish with him, then."

Hanson interrupted impatiently. "Your orders are to bring L'Heureux back to Paris for questioning. You can check with McFee on that."

"I will," Durell said. "But if he killed Orrin Boston, I wouldn't mind seeing him dead, myself."

"That's exactly how McFee said you'd feel. I spoke to him on the trans-Atlantic wire just an hour ago. He said you're to call him back on this. But L'Heureux has to be returned alive and talkative."

Durell lit a cigarette. There was a lull in the procession of manikins moving on the ramp. From somewhere there came a piped Piaf recording into the perfumed salon. Then a girl stepped out from behind the sequined stage curtain and began to walk down the ramp, heading toward them.

"Here is Madeleine," Brumont whispered.

"Where does she figure in this?" Durell asked.

"Madeleine works for us. She was assigned to L'Heureux long ago." Brumont smiled and ran a thumb apologetically along the pointed lapels of his coat. "Naturally, we keep an eye on your people just as you do with us. No apologies are necessary, eh? Madeleine Sardelle operated for us to gain L'Heureux' confidence. She did well. She reached his bed and became his mistress."

"But L'Heureux is now in Algeria."

"Yes, and she was there until last week, with him. Then he sent her back to Paris and she resumed her normal occupation here." Brumont looked thoughtful. "She left L'Heureux before Orrin Boston was killed, but she insists her subject is innocent. She is quite passionate about it, and I charged her with having fallen in love with L'Heureux. She admits this. Now I do not trust her, and it is unfortunate, because Madeleine was a fine operative for us. It is possible that, with a woman, loyalty

14

can be shifted because of emotional attachments. Madeleine set her own trap for L'Heureux, perhaps, and was caught in it herself. In any case, she must now be regarded as a double agent. She must be considered as having no sense of values where L'Heureux is concerned, yet we must continue to use her as if we trusted her. It is a dark and devious game we all play, m'sieu."

Durell looked closely at the girl. Madeleine Sardelle was a redhead, with wide brows and large gray eyes and a frightened mouth. Her cheekbones looked faintly Slavic. The fall suit of checked wool that she modeled hugged a long-legged, high-breasted Parisian figure. Her first few steps were graceful, and then she seemed to stumble and her hand moved hesitantly to the silk scarf at her throat. She looked quickly at Brumont, then her eyes touched Durell and lingered on him for a moment before jumping to the arched foyer entrance to the salon. A dark-faced man in a blue suit stood there, a raincoat over his arm. The girl's mouth opened and closed. Turning, to exhibit the clothing she modeled, and it seemed to Durell that she was trembling, but he couldn't be sure about it at this distance. From the corner of his eye he saw the green-haired Madame Sofie walk quickly toward the dark-faced man in the foyer entrance.

Brumont made a small sound. "A magnificent woman, non?"

"A very frightened girl," Durell muttered.

"Of course. She understands her danger."

"What is she afraid of?"

"If her first reports are true, L'Heureux played between rival factions of the Algerian rebels. Even here in Paris, they employ their gangster tactics, m'sieu. They murder, kidnap, terrorize. She has appealed to us for protection. It seems that L'Heureux not only crossed Monsieur Boston and your organization, but he also double-crossed the rebels in some way. We do not know the details. It will be up to you to ascertain them—that is, if you wish to go to Marbruk rather than wait for the situation to be clarified—"

Brumont suddenly interrupted himself and lurched to his feet. Madeleine Sardelle had halted in the white-carpeted circle at the foot of the ramp. She looked wildly at Brumont, and at the man in the foyer entrance still talking to Madame Sofie. Then she turned and ran back along the ramp to the curtained stage, plunging through

15

the velvet draperies with a backward glance of pure terror.

"Quickly," Brumont snapped.

Durell was already on his feet. The man in the foyer slapped Madame Sofie and turned to run out of the salon. Durell ignored him. He raced up the ramp to the curtained stage, while the small group of patrons stared at him in startled surprise. The curtains gave him a moment's trouble, and then he dove through them.

"Mlle. Sardelle!"

A frightened brunette in scanty lingerie stared at him in confusion and then pointed. "That way, m'sieu. Is she ill?"

Durell ran to his left. He heard a dim shouting from the salon beyond the curtains, but he didn't pause. From the wing of the stage, a corridor ran in both directions, lighted with low-power yellow bulbs. He yanked open the first door he came to and found himself stared at by four models in various stages of undress. The girls looked at him with cool, professional eyes in masked faces. He muttered an apology and said, "Mlle. Sardelle?"

"The second door to the right, m'sieu," one of the girls said. She took off her brassiere and turned her smoothly tanned back to him, but not very quickly. "She is always the lucky one, eh?"

Durell backed out and heard the girls laugh. He was almost at the second door down the hallway when he heard Madeleine Sardelle scream.

Chapter Three

GLASS CRASHED somewhere behind the solid panels of the dressing-room door. Durell tried the door knob, shoved hard with his shoulder. The door was locked. The girl screamed again, the sound ending in a quick sob of anguish and terror. Durell stepped back two paces and slammed at the door in a low crouch, hitting the panel just below the latch. It snapped with a splintering of wood, and the door slammed wildly backward as he drove inside.

As he crossed the threshold he dropped low, touching one hand to the floor.

His method of entry saved him from the wild shot

16

that came his way. The bullet went high into the corridor beind him. There were two men in the dressing room with Madeleine Sardelle, and the redheaded girl was struggling in the grip of the taller of the two, who had a hand clamped across her mouth to prevent another scream. The second one had the gun. With a glance, Durell saw there were no others on either side of the doorway. The girl must have thrown something at her attackers. She had missed and shattered the window behind her instead, and the man who held her was now trying to back off with her in that direction. There was no time to see any more.

The one with the gun wore a cap and a turtle-neck sweater of fuzzy gray wool that smelled of the rain and acrid sweat; his face was thin and sharp, a peculiar sallow brown as if he had been deeply tanned and was in the process of losing that tan because of indoor living. Or hiding. His eyes were wild. He tried to jump aside as Durell's momentum carried him into the room. The gun went off again, and again the shot went wide, and Durell caught him with stiff fingers rammed into his belly. The man grunted, and Durell chopped at his neck and sent him spinning against the lighted mirror on the wall. The gun hit the floor. The man's shoulder smashed the electric bulbs circling the mirror in a quick series of popping bursts of glass. Durell kept moving, spinning on his toes.

Madeleine still struggled in the second man's grip. She managed to bite the man's hand at the same moment that Durell tore her free. There was a scrambling sound behind him and something clubbed at his back. The wind went out of him. He heard a sharp command in Arabic. Durell pushed the girl aside and swung to face his assailants. Something slammed into his stomach and as he fought up again, the smaller of the two men picked himself up from among the broken mirror shards on the floor and shouted in a high, lisping voice. Again, Durell thought it was Arabic. Then both men moved toward him like darting snakes. He kicked at the first and his heel shattered bones in the man's face, but the other was equally adept at judo. A telegraph pole smashed into Durell's ribs and he went down. He tried to grab at the second man and failed. The other's face went dim and the room whirled and darkened as he fell. He saw the taller of the two kneel and help his companion to

17

his feet. He pushed up as both men crowded out through the broken window.

Georges Brumont ran into the dressing room a moment too late to stop them.

Durell's chest felt as if a ton of coal had been dropped on him. His throat burned as he drew a deep breath and pushed himself up from the floor. His hand was bleeding. Brumont barked questions at him and he waved to the window, but he didn't bother to go there himself. He looked at the Sardelle girl. The redhead was slumped on a pink-cushioned stool that somehow had survived the wreckage. Her head was bent forward in her hands, and her long hair screened her face.

Fred Hanson came in, followed by Madame Sofie. Brumont, with a gun in his hand, pushed them angrily out into the corridor.

Durell went to the girl. "Are you all right, mademoiselle?"

"Yes. *Merci.*"

"Sit still," he said. "You're quite safe now."

"Take care of yourself, m'sieu," she said. "You bleed."

Durell picked up a fragment of mirror and looked at himself. There was a shallow cut across his forehead. He wondered what his opponent had hit him with, but it wasn't worth trying to figure out. He saw a small wash-stand in a corner of the dressing room and he walked toward it, breathing with care because of the pain in his ribs. He turned on the tap. The water looked rusty. It felt luke-warm, but he put in the rubber stopper and let the basin fill and then he dunked his head in it. When he finished, he turned, bent forward to keep the water from dripping on his clothes, and the girl handed him a coarse towel.

"You may need a doctor, m'sieu."

"Hardly. You saw me in the salon with Brumont, didn't you?"

"Yes. It is you I am to talk to, according to Monsieur Brumont."

He nodded. "Durell is my name. Who were those men, and what did they want from you?"

The girl shrugged. She'd had time to partly strip off the trim woolen suit she had modeled in the salon, and her lingerie was black net over golden skin. Durel saw that her large gray eyes were tipped up at the outer

18

corners, not by a cosmetic effect but by a faintly Oriental cast to her features. The girl said, "They were Algerian terrorists."

"Why do they trouble you? You knew they were about, didn't you? You were afraid even when you came out on the stage earlier."

"I saw the one talking with Madame Sofie. The leader. His gang hangs out in a certain café I know. I went there often with—I knew who he was, that is all."

"You went to this café with Charles L'Heureux, you mean."

"Yes. It was my job. I was assigned to Charles L'Heureux."

"I understand." He looked at her deliberately, studying her figure. She seemed totally unconcerned about her partial nudity. He said quietly, "Put something on, please. Did Charley know these men?"

"Months ago, yes. Before he went back to Algiers."

"Was he very friendly with them?"

"It is all in my reports to Brumont, Mr. Durell. Charley said it was his job to be friendly with them. Just as you know from Brumont that it was my job to be friendly with Charley."

"Did L'Heureux ever tell you exactly what his job was?"

"He admitted he was an agent for your government. He knew I was assigned to him by Brumont. Once our cover identities were revealed, we had a good laugh over it all."

Durell felt in his pockets for a cigarette and decided not to smoke. His mouth felt swollen, but his ribs no longer ached. He dabbed at the cut on his forehead with the wet towel. The bleeding had stopped. He pushed back his thick, wet hair. The girl was lying, he decided. No matter what sort of a renegade L'Heureux might be, he wouldn't have casually told this girl of his job with Orrin Boston. He didn't like the sound of it. There was something evasive and difficult to define in the girl's manner.

"L'Heureux no longer has friendly contacts with these people, is that it?" he asked.

"They have sworn to kill him. He is on the rebels' black list."

"Why?"

She shrugged smooth, golden shoulders, looked down

19

at her hands on her bare knees. "It is a political situation. The rebels are devoted to terror and violence. Other Nationalist factions among the Moslems are willing to compromise with France, but the rebels refuse. They have embarked on a policy of assassination for anyone who dares discuss a settlement with Frenchmen. They fancy Charles did something bad to them, but you waste your breath if you ask me what it is. Brumont wished me to discover what Charles was up to, but I failed on that. Nothing works out as we wish it would, m'sieu."

"Their quarrel is with L'Heureux, not with you," Durell persisted. "Why should they attack you today like this?"

"They know me as Charles' *petite amie*." The girl's eyes were mocking, challenging. "They think I can lead them to Charles—as if I would." Her mouth curled scornfully. "I will not betray him, m'sieu, to them or to you."

"You're in love with him?"

"It is the way of the world, m'sieu. A woman in this business must be prepared to give herself to the enemy. In the shadows sometimes one finds truth, in mockery one is surprised to learn of sincerity. I let Charles have me, and I fell in love with him." Her eyes were level, candid. "I understand from Brumont that you are here to bring Charles back to Paris. To justice. He is not a criminal. I do not believe the charge against him. Perhaps my usefulness to Brumont is ended, but I am convinced of this as the truth. When Charles returns, he will protect me from any future attacks of these murderers."

Durell picked up a red flannel robe from the floor and handed it to her. "Your Charley won't be protecting anyone," he said. "He'll be in jail."

She shook her head and held the robe limply before her.

"You know what he did," Durell added. "He murdered my best friend. Please get dressed now."

She sat down on the pink stool again. She was good, Durell decided, very, very good. She had recovered outwardly from the shock of the attack by the two terrorists, and now she exhibited dismay and denial of his words. She began a swift defense of L'Heureux, then paused. Fear touched her eyes; she bit her lip and was silent. Durell was unable to evaluate his reaction to her.

Brumont and Hanson came back into the dressing room then. Brumont looked like a fat, dark porpoise after his chase in the rain. He touched his shaggy moustache with the middle finger of his left hand.

"No good. No good at all, M. Durell. They have flown. There are alleys and all sorts of rundown cafés and bistros only a few steps away. Monsieur Hanson thinks they got into a car, but I never laid eyes on them, myself." Brumont looked at Madeleine. "Do you know who they were, *cherie?*"

She shook her head. She still stared at Durell. "There are so many of them. I could not name these two in particular."

"I see." Brumont nodded. "Rest yourself, mademoi-selle, and be at ease. Monsieur Durell, may we speak privately?"

Durell followed the fat man out of the shattered dressing room. Brumont led the way back to the salon, where the customers were answering questions of two uniformed gendarmes. "This way," Brumont said and opened a door to Madame Sofie's private office.

"If Sofie works for you," Durell said, looking around the plush, feminine decor of rococo pink and gold, "this place is bugged to a fair-thee-well, I'll bet."

"Bugged, m'sieu?"

"You have microphones and tape recordings."

Brumont smiled blandly. "But of course. Your people do the same, do they not? But since the CIA and Paris Intelligence and the Deuxième Bureau have always maintained cordial relations and cooperate like true allies, there should be no objection." There was irony under the Frenchman's smile. "In any case, although we are in private here, you may guard your words as you will."

"You don't trust Hanson any more than I, then."

Brumont shrugged and chose a small, vile Italian cigar from a battered case and lit it with care. "It is not for me to criticize your Embassy personnel. Hanson means well, but he always has the women on his mind. Always. He is a young bull, and bulls must have their way, you understand. In any case, he is merely liaison man between your organization and mine."

"About Madeleine Sardelle," Durell suggested. "Was this attack on her a real one, or was it faked to throw our sympathy her way?"

"I do not know. L'Heureux might have arranged it, even from his prison cell in Marbruk. He plays both ends against the middle, as you say. An opportunist of the first water. It is unfortunate that in our business we sometimes find it expedient to recruit the rascals and rogues with expert knowledge of the local terrain, so to speak. Orrin Boston thought the good might outweigh the evil in hiring L'Heureux. We gave him our dossier on L'Heureux' activities but he went ahead and utilized him, anyway. You feel badly that L'Heureux murdered your friend, of course. And you have no wish to help L'Heureux. Yet your job is to go to Marbruk and bring him back to your Embassy here."

Durell's face was like stone. "I understand that."

"It is important that we learn what L'Heureux was up to." Brumont looked at his crooked Italian cigar. "He has played the rebels against the el-Abri forces in Marbruk—and it is our good fortune that both factions of the criminal rebel movement fight each other as much as they war against us. They are all gangsters, supplied by arms from Tunis and Cairo. They fight like savages, perpetrating medieval horrors against friendly Moslems and French settlers alike. I could tell you tales of their tortures, their adamant refusal to negotiate—" Brumont interrupted himself. "One loses one's perspective in emotion in this matter. I apologize, m'sieu."

"It is understandable. What do we do with the girl?"

"She will go with you to Algeria," Brumont said flatly. "We know that she is frightened and alone here in Paris. We know she is in love with your suspect, and hence not to be considered dependable. Perhaps this kidnap attempt—if it was that—may make her more reliable to us. She has been trustworthy in the past. Perhaps she will see the truth about her Charley, inevitably. You understand, I have not given her any cause to think we no longer trust her."

"But she's intelligent," Durell objected. "She must know she is suspect in your department now."

"Of course. It is a game we play."

"Then why not restrain her and keep her in Paris until I return with L'Heureux?" Durell asked.

"She is partly Algerian, you know. She will be useful, as long as you keep your eyes open and aware of her potential weakness. She has begged me to keep her on."

"She's partly Moslem?"

22

"Her father was a Legionnaire in the old days. Her mother was Algerian. She is a product of the *bidonvilles* —the native tin-can villages in the slums. But a beautiful product, as you have observed."

"Beautiful enough. Like a leopard in the night."

"And intelligent. She knows much about the rebels. But love makes a woman lose her perspective, unfortunately. In custody here in Paris, she reports nothing to us. Traveling with you, she may reveal much more. It will be like carrying a hot coal in your hand, but it may prove to be worth the price."

Durell matched the Frenchman's bland look. He sensed a sardonic note in the man's comments on cooperation, and remembering past cross-purposes of foreign policy, he wondered how far he could trust Deuxième Bureau in relation to the information he needed. The primary rule for any agent was to trust no one, accept nothing on face value, and be on guard against everything. Brumont was an old hand, an expert. Durell had no illusions about him, but he respected the man and liked him.

"I'll consult with my people about it," he said. "And find out if they really want L'Heureux returned here. For my part, your Army people in Marbruk can stand him up against a wall and shoot him out of hand, if the evidence is correct and he killed Boston."

"But we do not know anything for certain," Brumont objected. "And then we would lose what lies in L'Heureux' head about the rebels. You understand how important it is to know all we can about them."

Durell nodded. "The girl still troubles me, though."

"I have arranged passage for both of you on the plane leaving at seventeen hours for Algiers."

"Just what have you told her about me?"

"Only that you are L'Heureux' superior sent to investigate the serious charges against him. Nothing more."

"Even that may be too much."

Brumont spread his fat hands. "An intelligent woman must be given some grains of truth in the pill she must swallow."

"She will never trust me," Durell objected.

"No. Do not expect her to. It is the game we play, to become knowledgeable at the expense of the enemy. We lie, cheat, steal, and kill. We do these things as a bookkeeper does his additions every day."

23

Durell made no final decision. A gendarme knocked on the door and reported to Brumont that the search for the gunmen had failed. Durell returned to the main salon. The fashion show was over, and the big room was deserted. He lit a cigarette and touched the slightly pulsing bruise on his forehead. His head ached. It was one o'clock, and Deirdre would be waiting around the corner at Jacques' bistro.

He had more than one reason to visit Jacques, however.

Chapter Four

MADELEINE SARDELLE was waiting in her dressing room when he returned there. The girl had propped up one of the larger fragments of broken mirror and was combing her long red hair. She did not pause or turn when he entered. Her pale gray eyes met Durell's in the mirror and she nodded, and Durell closed the door behind him. She had changed into a slim tailored suit, and a tan raincoat was at hand.

He ignored his French. "Do you speak English, mademoiselle?"

"A little. Well enough, I think. Is it necessary?"

"It may be, later on."

She put away the comb and pursed her mouth to apply lipstick. "Brumont has told you all about me, I presume."

"Some of it. We are in the same business and we are to collaborate."

She moved her lips to smooth the lipstick. "You are not a stupid man. You know I am badly frightened. I wish to be out of this business, as you call it. Those men would have done unpleasant things to me, given the opportunity. They want to know about L'Heureux. Brumont no longer trusts me, I know. And I don't trust you. In a way, it is a fair enough basis for our mutual effort."

Durell smiled. "You're very frank."

"Do you think so?"

"Not really. A fine actress, let's say."

She laughed, stood up, and took his arm. "Then we are agreed. You distrust me. I distrust you. I am not

24

very fond of Americans, you know. I saw too many of them, years ago, in Africa. You expect me to—what is it, double-cross? Yes. And you take me for a foolish woman who is in love with the wrong man. You condescend toward me. But perhaps for the moment we can arrange a truce. You *are* taking me to Marbruk, are you not?"

"If you wish."

"I am ordered there by Brumont. It will be interesting to have you as a traveling companion and—collaborator?"

"Let's call it a truce until the plane, then. At five o'clock."

They went out into the hallway. The two policemen on duty there stepped aside to let them leave. Durell was very conscious of the girl's spectacular beauty. He was also aware of the wire-tight condition of her nerves. Under her smile were taut little muscles and faint smudges that cosmetics couldn't hide.

"Do you mind," she said, "if we stay together until we are on the plane? I have a few things to pack—you may come up to my flat—and perhaps we could have an *apéritif* and lunch together."

"I have a date waiting for me at Jacques' place," he said.

"A girl?"

"My girl, yes."

"An American?"

"Yes."

"This complicates things for you." She laughed. "Perhaps it would be embarrassing for you if I went with you, but I promise—"

"It will be all right," Durell decided.

The cool August rain still fell over Paris. A mist hung over the Seine, obscuring the bridges and the Notre Dame spires, softening the walks and statues and stone stairways going down to the river bank. A man in a black beret leaned over the stone balustrade, staring at the dappled surface of the river, and when they passed by, Durell heard him straighten and saunter after them as they walked to the first crossing. He decided the black beret was Brumont's agent, and he would have to be more than usually careful at Jacques' place.

The café was a short walk from the river, on a narrow cobbled street edged with dripping trees. A striped awning sheltered the tables outside. Three men were

25

visible within, at the zinc-topped bar, and through the shutter door they could be heard arguing volubly about taxes. Deirdre Padgett sat alone at a table on the sidewalk under the awning.

As always, Durell's heart lurched when he first glimpsed her, and all his resolutions to keep her out of his life grew dimmer. He knew her intimately. There were no secrets between them except those of his work, and she had come to accept this, even if she refused to understand it. Her raven hair was touched by the soft mist, and she wore a small suede beret. Her winged brows were inquiring as she saw Durell approach with Madeleine on his arm.

"Sam. . . ."

He kissed her and drew a chair for Madeleine and introduced the two girls. Deirdre was cool and aloof; then her eyes warmed again as she touched Durell's hand.

"Were you waiting long?" he asked.

"I only just got here, darling. You never waste time, do you?"

He laughed. "You mean Madeleine? She's part of the job I came here to do."

"Not very distasteful work, is it?" Deirdre asked. "Or am I making unpleasant noises. I thought we were going to have the afternoon together. Alone, I mean." She picked up her small glass of vermouth. She wore a pale gray dress trimmed with white piping, under a transparent rain cape. "I suppose I should be used to this by now. But I'm downright jealous about anything where you are concerned."

"I'm sorry, Dee. There's no need to be."

"Should I trust you?"

"No." He grinned. "Definitely not."

Madeleine spoke in her throaty French. "Please do not be disturbed by my presence, mademoiselle. Monsieur Durell is only interested in protecting me and convicting my friend of murder."

Deirdre looked quickly at Durell. "Something you can talk about, darling?"

"No," he said.

"We travel as custodian and prisoner," Madeleine added, "although neither wishes to admit to the relationship. I am a foolish woman who chose to fall in love with one who may be considered the enemy. But not

26

by me. I shall never agree. But in any case, you may forget about me, mademoiselle, if you wish."

Durell said, "If you ladies plan to use your claws, go right ahead and help yourself. I think I'll have a word with Jacques about lunch. Excuse me."

He went into the café to where the three Frenchmen were arguing at the bar. Through the dim window he saw the man in the black beret hovering at the corner. Jacques, a dark obsidian mass behind the bar, simply nodded to Durell and went on talking to his customers. Durell finally asked to consult with Madame Jacques about the lunch he wished to order.

"Of course, m'sieu. In the kitchen, if you will."

He went through a curtained archway to the rear of the café. There wasn't much time, with Deirdre and Madeleine outside and Brumont's shadow on the corner. It would have to be quickly and naturally.

A hallway painted a queasy brown led into the kitchen. Madame Jacques looked up from her cast-iron coal stove and nodded. She was stout, gray, and mustached. "Up the stairs, m'sieu."

Durell turned up a narrow flight of enclosed steps to the floor above. At the top of the stairway was a green door, and he rapped on it in a quick, simple signal. Footsteps approached from the other side and it was opened.

"Hello, Hal."

"Welcome to Ears West."

They shook hands. Hal Remington was a middle-aged expatriate who looked more Parisian than the New Yorker he had originally been. A poet and an artist, he had come to Paris in the late Twenties when a large colony of Americans had made it their adopted residence. Remington had a short, forked beard, a flat face, and bright intelligent eyes under bushy gray brows. He looked rather like an aging and sardonic Mephistopheles, gone a bit to seed. The room was a rat's nest, cluttered with two studio easels, clothing scattered everywhere, and unfinished canvases stacked heavily against the plastered walls. There was a huge desk with an ancient Oliver No. 9 typewriter standing among a heap of squeezed-out tubes of pigment. A wardrobe closet stood open, and in the bottom section, built into a drawer, was a compact and powerful radio transmitter and receiver. On the window ledge that overlooked the cobbled street, two wet pigeons huddled and argued for space beside a pair of high-powered binoculars.

Durell looked out the window and discovered he could see the front entrance of Madame Sofie's salon.

"Quite a view," he said. "Comfortable here, Hal?"

"I get some work done. And Madame Jacques has graduated from the Cordon Bleu kitchens." Remington kissed paint-stained fingertips. "At last, after fifty-odd years, I find myself at peace with the stomach. I am never hungry. As a matter of fact, *amigo*, I grow fat sitting up here like a spider in one of your webs." Remington looked out of the window, too. "One of Brumont's boys followed you here. That all right?"

"Don't underestimate the Deuxième Bureau," Durell said. "They watch us and pick up tips from American tourists at Madame Sofie's. And they know we watch them, in turn, from here. Friendly rivalry for now. Anyway, it wouldn't surprise me if Jacques takes a pay check from Brumont as well as from our Embassy. Nice, clean competition."

"As long as we're allies," Remington said.

Durell's eyes darkened. "Let's hope that never changes."

Remington lit a Gauloise. "Business has been slow, you know. I've even done two paintings this month. Only two couriers through last week, and a couple of cut-out assignments. I used to think your business had a lot of excitement in it, Sam, but so far it's been a bloody bore. But the pay is good and I'm getting fat, as I said. You're here about Orrie Boston, aren't you?"

Durell nodded and sat down. "What do you have on him, Hal?"

"Orders for you, somewhere." Remington rummaged through the rubbish on his huge desk. "Came in by code from Washington two hours ago. Yours not to reason why, friend, yours just to do or die."

"Don't be so cheerful. Let's have it."

"You are to bring Charles L'Heureux back alive," Remington said.

"No matter what?"

"No matter what."

"Suppose he's really guilty? Suppose he killed Orrie?"

"We think he did. I'm sorry, Sam. That's the word we got from Marbruk. I knew Orrin Boston, too, don't forget. We had some high old times every time he made it into Paris."

28

"You'd better brief me on the background," Durell said. "What I got from Brumont may be out of perspective. There's a girl involved in it, too—one whom Brumont uses but doesn't trust. I have to take her on."

Remington nodded and chuckled. "The Sardelle. She snuggled up to our Charley and liked what she found between the sheets."

"Anything on her I could use?"

"No. About L'Heureux, he's important because of what he knows. Washington thinks he can be made to talk if he's pulled out of Algeria, where every rebel group wants to ventilate him a bit and maybe carve off special pieces of anatomy. Our Sardelle would be heart-broken if that happened." Remington ran fingers through his forked gray beard. "You've been in North Africa before, haven't you?"

"With the old Lincoln Unit of the OSS. Making ready for the landings at Algiers," Durell said.

Remington dragged at his cigarette. "Two angles to this, but they both tie to friend Charley. You know how it is sometimes, a man in the field has to make use of whatever human material is at hand. Orrie Boston found our Charley popping up in his work and finally put him on the payroll to keep an eye on him. Did Brumont give you a rundown on L'Heureux?"

"There were a number of G.I.'s who turned adventurer in the Mediterranean area after the war," Durell said.

"And on the surface, all of them good patriots." Remington nodded. "Modern-day buccaneers to some people. Looters, smugglers, murderers, dope-runners to others. L'Heureux was all of the latter and then some." Remington's light tone was belied by the hardness of his bright eyes. "L'Heureux probably was running guns to the rebels when Orrie contacted him. Any chance to talk to the rebels has to be seized on—they resist contact and demand prior independence like a bunch of fanatics. Anyway, Orrie figured that our Charley was playing off two factions of the rebels against each other. Brumont wants chapter and verse on all that. He expects to get it, when you deliver L'Heureux to Paris. We'll cooperate on that. As for Washington, your K Section wants to wash its own dirty linen and take L'Heureux apart for information and then suitable penalties—when he's been squeezed dry."

"Just what was Orrie working on?"

"His last report was optimistic. He'd been in contact with Hadji el-Abri. Negotiating a compromise conference with the French Army. Unheard of, these days. If L'Heureux hadn't killed him, maybe the rebels would have done the job. The rebels won't allow any parley."

"You seem damned sure L'Heureux killed Orrie."

"We've got the commandant's report, that's all."

"And the motive?"

"Two points, possibly. One, Orrie got the dope on the game our Charley was playing and faced L'Heureux with it. Or maybe L'Heureux took our pay and a check from the rebels, too, and got word to stop Orrie Boston from meddling and playing the part of the neutral intermediary."

"And second?"

"Second, and much more specific, is a matter of over two hundred grand in American currency, lifted off a courier of ours in Cairo four weeks ago."

Durell was startled. "I didn't hear about that."

"Nobody has. It was money from another section—not itemized in the national budget, you can be sure—and it's being sorely missed. At the time, there was that regular crisis in the Mideast, you remember, and people recommended stepping lightly. No protests were made aside from routine remonstrance to the police, and nobody mentioned anything so mundane as a quarter of a million American dollars."

"I gather it was traced to Algeria," Durell said drily.

"Right. Via our friend Charley."

"He hijacked our own man?"

"Not personally. He was here in Paris then. Doing some odds and ends for the rebel terrorists in metropolitan France, we think. That's how Madeleine got put onto him."

"Then what ties L'Heureux to the missing money?"

"We don't know, but Orrie Boston did, and maybe that's why L'Heureux killed him. It will be up to you to get to the bottom of that one, too."

"And the missing money?"

"It would be nice to get it back, I'm told."

"No idea where it is?"

"Sure. Algeria."

"With the rebels?"

"With L'Heureux, we think."

Remington crushed out his cigarette. He used a pink

ceramic bowl that looked remarkably and repulsively organic. "Algeria is important to us, Sam, because it's part of the tug-of-war between East and West. What *we* would like is a peaceful, amicable solution that will suit both the French and the Algerians. It's not our business to meddle here. But a man like L'Heureux, with the morality of an alley cat, can do everybody much damage. Right now he's in a hot little cell in an outpost in Marbruk. He knows a lot about the rebels that we don't know, and intelligence on it is vital to both the French and to us. So bring him back."

"I wish they'd send somebody else. If he killed Orrie—"

"One other thing. That quarter-of-a-million in cool green American currency, in the hands of the rebels might be hard to explain to Brumont and his people."

"Does he know about it?"

"No. One little item we managed to keep from him." Remington's eyes were shrewd. "L'Heureux has to be brought back with his tongue wagging. I know you wouldn't mind seeing him dead, Sam. So would I. It's a rough deal, because much as you'd like to break his neck, you'll have to protect him from a couple of thousand enemies every inch of the way. The French over there blame him for the Marbruk massacre. The rebels want their hands on him because of some double-cross—probably the money matter. But you wrap him up in cotton wool and deliver him to the Embassy and Brumont. Those are your orders."

"Is the military situation in Marbruk really tough?"

"Couldn't be worse. The French military there are remote, isolated, no men to spare, especially since the rebels are running their offensive all along the Tunisian frontier. Nobody can be spared at the moment. We could wait a few days, of course, for the area to come back under control—it's bubbling like a witch's cauldron, right now —but you can get in and poke around, meanwhile."

"All right," Durell said. "Is that all?"

"Isn't it enough?"

Durell nodded. "Thanks for nothing."

He went downstairs through Madame Jacques' kitchen and reached the front of the café a few moments later. He had been absent only ten minutes. He had left Deirdre and Madeleine at their table, eyeing each other like uninhibited jungle cats. Now they sat side by side, and the redheaded model was holding a handkerchief to her eyes while Deirdre patted her and made soothing sounds of consolation.

Both girls looked at Durell as if he were the common enemy. Madeleine Sardelle smiled first.

Chapter Five

FAR BELOW was the Mediterranean, black and fathomless. The Air France plane to Algiers droned smoothly southward after its single stop at Marseilles. Madeleine Sardelle leaned back in her seat with her head pressed against the cushioned chair. Her eyes appeared to be closed, but they were not. From under the dark fan of her lashes she watched Durell, seated beside her. His face was in repose. A calm and dangerous man, this one, she thought. It would not be easy to fool him. He seemed quick and competent—and handsome, too. Something stirred in her as she thought about him, and she was annoyed with herself. When would she ever change? Those days were over, when a man—any man—meant someone to conquer and use and then discard. Charley was the last of a long series of faces she had known in passion and secret contempt.

Soon it would all be changed, she thought gratefully. She had picked the right one at last, in L'Heureux. If all went well—and it was her job to see that it went smoothly—then the past would be buried and forgotten. There would be South America, the warmth and luxury of all the money they would ever need for the rest of their days. True, Charley might prove to be a bore; he was such a brute, so uncouth; but time would take care of that. She decided not to worry about anything in the future that was not specific.

She had grown up in a hard, bitter school. She was going home now, but there was no happiness in the thought. Quite the contrary. She could remember back through the twisted years to her father, that huge man with his moustache, his Legionnaire's uniform. And her mother, meek and veiled, a Moslem who had abandoned her people to live with a Frenchman. There were many memories afloat on the sea of her mind like drifting bits of debris. After her father had left them, her mother went home to her village with Madeleine, and they lived on the grudging bounty of an uncle, a local fisherman. When Madeleine was twelve, she had been sold to a friend of her uncle's for the price of a new length of anchor rope. That was one night she would never forget. That was the night when the curtain was torn and she made the vows by which she had lived ever since.

Fortunately, she had inherited French looks and a figure from her father. The war years were only a tangled skein of memories, but the Americans who remained in Africa afterward had been a lucrative source of income. She learned English along with diversified arts of love; she learned to sing and dance in the nightclubs of Algiers; she came to use men and learned to Europeanize herself until no one guessed her origins.

Thinking of this, she watched Durell from under the delicate arcs of her lashes. Brumont knew all the details of her life, and she wondered how much had been told to this silent man. She was a little afraid of Durell. He seemed different, more remote. She would have to be careful, she thought again.

Odd about Charley. She had already heard about the big American, the wild one, the Happy One, in the months when she had moved in rebel circles on orders from Brumont. Brumont had given her the job because of the facts in her dossier; there had been long interviews at offices in the Deuxième Bureau; she had convinced them of her patriotism, her love for France.

Madeleine laughed silently. All that mattered was money and Brumont paid well. It was easy enough to contact L'Heureux. It pleased her vanity to play both ends of the game, and it paid well. It paid even better after that night on the beach at Nice, on that holiday they took together, she playing the part of an innocent type, a *petite* from Madame Sofie's salon. She had gotten Charley drunk and let him think he had taken her by force after that struggle in the water, near the rocks. It had been amusing to let him tear the Bikini off her, to let him think he was the master. Now she was sure that Charley was in love with her. Her own feelings were confused. When she thought of him deeply, she felt fear, more than anything else. She never knew what he was thinking. She was more afraid of Charley by far than of this man beside her in the plane.

But Charley had the money. And money was the future.

33

Things had gone wrong because Charley'd had to kill that man, Orrin Boston, and he was in military custody now. But she had received his message by courier last night. He wanted her to accompany the agent being sent to take him back to Paris. The money waited for them out in the desert, amid the wild *jebels* of the south. She would help Charley to escape. Nothing could stop them.

"Madeleine," Durell said quietly.

She opened her eyes wide, hearing his voice above the drone of the plane's engines. "Yes, m'sieu."

"A penny for your thoughts."

Panic touched her. Could he read her mind? "I was thinking of the American girl you introduced me to. Is she your fiancée?"

"In a way."

"She is very lovely. And very sympathetic."

"One of her endearing faults," Durell said. "But you were not thinking about Deirdre. Charley is on your mind, right?"

She persisted with Deirdre, clinging to the subject. "Are you in love with Miss Padgett, m'sieu?"

"I think so, yes."

"Then she is a lucky woman, I think."

"She's on her way back to the States. And I'm here with you."

Madeleine opened her pale eyes wide. She turned her face toward him as they sat side by side on the double seat, and in turning this way, her leg moved and her thigh pressed his. "Is there significance in what you have just said?"

He met her smile. "I have my faults, too. And you and I understand each other. We are in the same business. We know the dangers of the world and its few pleasures, too, perhaps."

"You know that I am in love with my Charles."

"Tell me about him, then," Durell said.

"There is nothing to tell. Brumont made it plain what a woman's role must be in this business of yours."

"The obvious one," Durell said.

"Yes. So I became the woman of Charles L'Heureux, in order to become his confidant, so to speak. Does that shock you?"

"Not really."

"And I fell into the trap of my own making."

"I'm not so sure of that," Durell said.

34

"But I do love him. And I believe in his innocence."

"You know what he is. You know the crimes he has committed. An adventurer, fattening on a troubled world."

"But not a murderer," Madeleine said flatly.

"How can you be sure?"

"When a woman lives with a man, she comes to know his capacities for matters other than love. If he is considered such a terrible man, why did your Mr. Boston take him into the service as an agent in the first place?"

"We compromise when we have to. L'Heureux is perhaps the only American on the scene who knows as much about the rebels as he does. Orrin Boston heard about him and chose to use him."

"So you think my Charles killed him. But I will help Charles, if I can. You must understand that."

"There will be no help for him, if he killed Orrin."

"We shall see," Madeleine said quietly.

Durell looked at his watch. Africa, the bright city of Algiers, and the airport at Maison Blanche was just over the horizon of night.

Chapter Six

THE COMMAND POST of the *chasseur* unit stationed at Marbruk occupied a stone farmhouse on the lower slope of the *jebel* overlooking the valley. The farm had been a prosperous one, thanks to irrigation here on the fringes of the southern desolation. It had been owned by a René St. Leger, a wealthy Frenchman whose family had grown olives, and grapes for the strong Algerian wines, for three generations. René had been knifed in the back while patrolling the town with his territorial unit of home guards two months ago, and Captain DeGrasse had occupied the farm when the rest of St. Leger's family, wife and two daughters, moved into their villa at Algiers.

Aside from the main farmhouse, there were two stone barns, and in the northernmost of the barns, half a mile from the house itself, was the military prison. Two or three outhouses formed a cluster suitable for both defense and internal control.

At nine o'clock, Charley L'Heureux slipped a small wad of hundred-franc notes to the private who guarded his

35

cell in what had been the hayloft and accepted a bottle of cognac in return. A hot wind blew through the barred windows of his room, and sand hissed and moved along the wooden floor. He could feel it against his bare ankles, like the stinging bites of a thousand gnats.

"*Mon ami*," L'Heureux said to the guard, "a thousand thanks. This will save my life."

"Nothing can save your life. Not the life of a traitor." The guard was a thin, tired man from St. Nazaire, and he was homesick and fed up with Algeria and the rebels. Nothing he had seen since he had been drafted could explain to his clerical mind what he was doing here. "And I am not your friend, understand?"

"Who did I betray?" L'Heureux asked. "No one but myself, Pepi."

"One grows philosophical in jail, that is a fact."

"Look here," Charley insisted. "I'm not French, am I?"

"You have a French name."

"But I'm an American. I was born in Arostuga, Maine, U. S. A."

"Then you are a traitor to your country, too," Pepi said. He had a tommy gun slung by its strap over his neck and nestled against his belly. "I do not wish to discuss it with you. I spit on you."

"Yet you take my money."

"At home I am an accountant, and I know that money is money," Pepi said. "It's all good and all bad, and I'm not a philosopher about money. One has no choice. It is needed."

"What will they do to me, Pepi? Have you heard?"

"If I had my way," the guard said, "we would do to you as the rebels did to the people of Marbruk. One fights fire with fire; it is as simple as that, to my mind. They kill and torture and mutilate. It is no better fate than you deserve."

"But the captain will not have me shot at dawn, eh?"

The guard shrugged. "No, and I am sickened to have to relieve your mind of that."

The guard moved away, climbing down the steps to the stone floor of the huge barn. Charley listened to his footsteps die away, standing in an attitude of acute attention. Finally he heard only the endless rattle of the wind and the hiss of sand blown in through the window. He went back to the cot with the cognac bottle.

He was a big man with powerful shoulders. His curly

36

blond hair was cropped short over a broad, weathered face. His eyes were greenish, reflecting hard and ugly things. He had seen too much of North Africa, for too long. He had heavy brows that were black in contrast to his pale, boyish hair. His khaki shirt was open down to the waist, and the hair on his chest was also dark. His khaki trousers were ragged and sweaty, torn at the cuffs. His sandals were cracked. He looked at his hands around the cognac bottle, big, strong hands that had helped him out of many a bad corner. But he couldn't remember as tight or bad a corner as this.

He wanted to laugh and curse all at once. He had reached down low this time, really low; but he saw himself as if crouching in the dirt only for the final spring to the top, to ultimate success.

He wondered if Madeleine had gotten his message. Better to do without her in this—for that matter, he'd like to forget her entirely, since he was tired of her and looked upon her as an Arab mongrel, hardly fit for the life he planned ahead. And he still didn't trust her fully, knowing she was Brumont's agent. Still, he needed her now. She could misdirect the agent coming for him, like a magician's assistant on stage. And even if it were only for a moment, it would be a crucial moment. The time for escape, and that would be enough.

Charley sighed, thinking how he would have to take Madeleine with him for a short time, anyway. Until he found another woman, perhaps. He wasn't constituted to lead a monogamist life for long.

He lay back on his hard cot and drank from the cognac bottle, then fished in his ragged shirt pocket for a Gauloise cigarette. Only three left now. Tomorrow would be the last round of the game. It was too bad that Orrin Boston's suspicions about the money and el-Abri had forced his hand prematurely. But it would work out all right. You had to learn to improvise, because the only thing certain in this world was that everything was uncertain.

The wind blew steadily through the window. Sand scratched at the floor. Charley turned his body toward the wall. Against his wish, he remembered the pine woods of Maine and his boyhood in the Thirties. The old man's potato farm went under the auctioneer's gavel, the quarry job had finally killed him, and the years on relief after that were no things of joy for a kid to remember. There wasn't much for a growing boy to do in those days. Occasionally he got a job as guide for New York hunters who tossed him tips like throwing bones to a dog. You went hungry often, and you fed yourself on hatred, which could keep you warm. And after a while the hatred filled your belly like a hot and satisfying meal.

Later, in the war, he already knew how to take care of himself and make a good thing out of what others regarded as nothing. In the confusion of North Africa, he saw a future untroubled by law or morality. It had taken time, and there were dead men on the trail behind him; but the end was now in sight. Charley smiled thinly in the gloom of his cell. It wouldn't be the end the Hadji el-Abri hoped for him, or what the agent, whoever he was, would want when he came for him.

He sat up abruptly when he heard the gunfire. It came in sharp and spiteful echoes on the wind, snapping irritably on the southern flanks of the town. First a rifle cracked, then the rattle of a tommy gun followed, then more rifles, and finally the dull thumping of grenades. Charley moved to the window as footsteps pounded through the stone barn. Hoarse shouts and yells came from the compound outside. Floodlights blossomed into bright, glaring eyes that scanned the night with the wild insanity of a madman. From the window, Charley saw the first red flicker of fire on the southern edge of town. A jeep motor roared into life, then several trucks raced out through the gates to the road below.

Charley swallowed a sudden dryness in his throat. It could be el-Abri out there, with his Kabyle guerrillas. They wanted him. Or it could be el-Abri's rivals, another guerrilla faction. In either case, he had cause to fear, although fear was not in him normally. It was this cell, he told himself. Being trapped if the rebel raid swept this far. He turned and yelled angrily as several *chasseurs* pounded down the steps outside, their equipment clinking, tommy guns in their hands. None of the soldiers paid any attention to him. He returned to the cell window and gripped the bars hard. The gunfire was reaching into the heart of Marbruk now, coming this way up the slopes of the *jebel*, into the ruined vineyards and orchards of the farms. It was a strong, bold raid, and the thin company of French troops would have their hands full.

Charley was suddenly sure that the wild desert men out there in the hot night were stabbing directly for him.

38

Jane Larkin heard the gunfire with a sudden quickening in her almost like relief. From the window of her room in the only hotel Marbruk could boast, she heard the thud of grenades and the hoarse shouts of frightened people in the market place below. She leaned out through the narrow window, but the mud streets were confused and dark, and all she glimpsed were running figures in flapping robes and *kachabias*. Jane breathed a little more quickly, her lips parted. Her boredom was forgotten.

"Jane, honey," Chet said. "Please get away from there."

She turned to look at her husband, petulant anger changing to scorn when she saw Chet loading a revolver as he sat on the edge of the huge bed. "What do you think you can with that?"

"You can't tell what's happening out there," he said.

"It's the rebels, raiding," she said impatiently.

"I know that. And there's a chance they'll break in here."

"So you plan to defend me?"

"I'll try, Jane," he said quietly.

"You could have taken me away days ago."

"It wasn't possible. You know how it's been."

She spoke spitefully. "Yes, but I didn't know how it would be when you sent for me, when I was with Daddy in Houston. You made it all sound so romantic. So desert-sheikish. You didn't have the nerve to tell me how filthy it really was."

Chet Larkin finished loading the .38 Smith & Wesson and put it on the bed beside him. His brown eyes were tired, candid, and patient. "Can you blame me for wanting you with me, Jane? Maybe I'm selfish, but I love you, honey, and I missed you so damned much I told a few lies to get you to join me here. I didn't think you'd find it so bad, though. Not really. I thought you might get to like it."

"Like it?" She thinned her mouth. She smoothed her hands down her hips. "We're likely to get killed by those crazy people."

"They probably won't get this far. It's just another raid."

He didn't want to go on arguing. This thing between them went beyond words, and he looked away from the anger and petulance in her face. He hadn't dreamed Jane would be like this. When he'd sent for her, he didn't think she'd find it all so bad, or that she'd be so helpless, and

39

disinterested in everything around her. The only thing she fastened her attention on was the heat, the dirt, the minor discomforts of joining him here until his contract ran out with Davide et Fils. Should have left her in Algiers, he thought. She liked the plush St. George Hotel. She'd enjoyed that day at the salmon-colored basilica of Notre Dame d'Afrique, high on Mt. Bouzaréa above the city. She'd liked Algiers, the sense of wartime excitement, the shops and cafés and milk bars and green-bereted paratroopers on security duty. Asking her to join him in provincial Marbruk was a mistake.

He had even entertained the dim hope that she could be persuaded to his renewing the contract. Davide was willing to make him chief of the geophysical crews, prospecting for oil out of Hassi Messaoud. Things were getting better out there. Lots of the oil riggers and prospecting engineers had their families with them, living in the prefab air-conditioned huts. The steel cabins were comfortable enough, with running water, electric lights, food trucked in from Algiers. And every fourth week you got flown back to Algiers for free for a week of rest. Lots of other guys made it with their wives.

But it hadn't worked that way. Jane said no, flatly and definitely, in total outrage. She wanted to go home to Houston.

They'd been married only a year when Chet got this chance to work with the oil exploration teams in the Sahara with this affiliate of the Société Francaise des Petroles. Jane was even more beautiful and more desirable now than she was when he first met her in Texas. He'd recognized from the first that her money and his need to carve a career for himself might come into serious conflict. But Jane always had refused to discuss it, laughing it off. And the first months had passed in a series of climactic ecstacies that gradually pushed his worries into the background. He'd always been a worrier, he thought, too reserved and conservative. But living with Jane should have made him aware of her personality flaws, whatever the joys and carelessness of her ways. If he'd been more alert, he wouldn't have sent for her, and then this hopeless break might never have come about.

He had to admit his own weakness. He'd have done anything to avoid a showdown with her, to keep her on any terms. But he'd lost her. Jane held him in contempt now—not for anything special, but simply because he had brought her into the discomforts and dangers of rebellious Algeria. She thought he was selfish and cruel. He merely loved her.

He watched her move back now, shrinking from the louder bursts of gunfire moving into the squalid town among the native *mechtas*. She lit a cigarette and hugged her arms across her breasts, cupping one elbow in the palm of her left hand. She was as tall as he, with long blond hair shining softly in the dim glow of the single lamp in the room. Still beautiful, he thought. He would never stop wanting her. But the last time they had enjoyed uninhibited love-making had been at the St. George in Algiers, after he'd met her plane at the Maison Blanche airport. That was two months ago. Watching her proud body in the thin negligee she wore, he wanted her now, this moment, ignoring the heat and danger that glittered in the night air. If she would only smile, he thought, she could name her own terms for the rest of their lives.

"Jane, please sit down. And maybe you ought to get dressed."

"Why? Where would we go?"

"It would be better if you were dressed," he said.

"You mean one of the natives might rape me?"

"Don't call them natives," he said. "Don't condescend toward them. It's their country."

"You know what they are," she said angrily. "Since when did you develop such a love for these dirty people?"

"They're not all the same. They need help. Try to understand them."

"They're killing and looting right now, aren't they? Just like a lot of savages."

"They're fighting for something they want. Independence, freedom, equality—maybe they don't know what it is themselves. Maybe they're going about it the wrong way. They make mistakes, but so do the French. Don't condemn them for trying." He watched Jane drag angrily at her cigarette. "Look, the French commander will be here any minute, I'm sure. DeGrasse promised he'd make arrangements to get us to the coast tomorrow. The raid may hold him up, but he'll show up soon. Try to control yourself, will you? Try not to find fault with everyone you meet here. This isn't Texas, don't forget, and your father is a long way off, in Houston. Throwing tantrums won't buy us anything."

Her mouth was jeering. "And until the Marines arrive,

41

you have your gun, is that it? Chet Larkin. My hero."

He didn't reply. He put the revolver aside, listening to the alarming rattle of a machine gun that seemed to be firing from directly under their second-floor window. From one of the dark alleys across the market place, a man began to scream in a high, ululating voice. The sound of agony made Jane suck in her breath sharply. Her face went pale. The gun rattled again. Two slugs slashed through the narrow curtained window. The thin material puffed inward as if slapped by someone's hand. Plaster chipped from the walls. Chet jumped for Jane and threw her to the floor and covered her with his body.

She breathed erratically under his weight. No more shots came. Their faces were close together, and Chet could see the bright, excited luminosity of her gray eyes looking up at him. They were the eyes of a total stranger.

Chapter Seven

THE TELEPHONE rang. It sounded abrupt and shrill in the big room. Chet felt Jane wriggle impatiently under him, trying to release herself from his weight. "Let me up," she said.

He rolled aside. The telephone kept ringing on the taboret beside the big bed. The square outside was silent now. The whole town was plunged into a sudden, unearthly quiet, in which the only sound was the imperative ring of the phone. Chet walked across the room and picked it up.

"Monsieur Larkin? One moment, please."

He lowered the telephone to his chest and looked at Jane. "It's the French commandant. Are you all right?"

"Just a bit bruised from your gallant gesture," Jane said.

"The fighting seems to have stopped."

Jane examined a broken fingernail. "I want a drink."

"Help yourself."

"Where is it?"

He gestured toward the bottle of Martel near the *bidet* in the corner, and Jane moved toward it, pushing up her thick yellow hair at the nape of her neck. Chet put the phone to his ear again as a voice began to rattle in the receiver. "Yes?"

"My apologies, m'sieu. Captain DeGrasse. We have been busy, you understand? I may not be able to see you to discuss your travel plans."

"What goes on with this raid?"

"It is being contained. I think you are quite safe where you are. But you must remain at the hotel. Under no circumstances are you or your wife to go into the streets until you hear from me again."

"When do we get out of here, captain?"

"I had hoped to arrange a military convoy to take you by truck to Algiers tomorrow. But I find myself unable to spare enough men. However, a liaison plane is due any moment with an American who is to take a prisoner back to France. I think I can arrange with him to take you and Madame Larkin on the plane first thing in the morning."

"That will be fine," Chet said. "I certainly appreciate it."

"You are all right? You have not been injured?"

"No, of course not."

"You sound rather strange, m'sieu."

"It's nothing. Thank you, captain."

"Remain at the hotel. I will call again directly when the plane lands."

Chet hung up. Jane was pouring a second drink of the Martel brandy. Her back was toward him. He got up and his shoes crunched on the plaster gouged from the walls by the two machine-gun slugs that had entered the room. He pulled the curtains tight over the window embrasure and put on another lamp. At least the town's power plant hasn't been knocked out yet, he thought.

"DeGrasse says there's a plane coming in soon," he told Jane. "We can leave on it in the morning."

"About time," she said.

He stood behind her, facing a small rococo mirror that reflected their images as Jane took another swallow of the brandy. He looked chunky and graceless beside her. When Jane had agreed to marry him, he had thought it a miracle of good fortune. He wasn't particularly good-looking, although his square features had a clean ruggedness. His dark hair looked thick and unkempt at the moment. His quiet, patient manner bordered almost on shyness, and this had caught Jane's attention first, that day when her father gave that cocktail party at the Houston ranch and he had been invited, in a patronizing gesture to the hired help, along with the other engineers. Jane's father had a financial interest in Davide et Fils, and Chet had already applied for a job with the geophysical exploration team due to go into the Sahara.

Jane gave him special attention because he had been the most reserved of the lot. Perhaps it intrigued her to draw him out. Certainly neither had expected the explosive attraction that built up between them during those next hours. Jane was bored, and Chet was something new to her. She was accustomed to flattery and adulation from many men, and Chet was different. Honest, she thought, and sincere. He was in love with her from the start. Because of what she was and what her money represented, he had stepped back until it was impossible to keep silent. Two weeks after they met, when he had seen her every day—usually at her demand—he asked her to marry him. And she had accepted.

His trip to Sahara had been postponed for months while he worked in her father's Houston offices. But he didn't want to think about that time now. In self-defense, he had insisted on going into the field, and Jane had joined him after a two-month delay.

It had taken just one year and two months, he thought bitterly, to turn them from impassioned lovers to enemies, coming together now only to claw and hurt one another. Well, he was surrendering. Giving up his one chance to break free and stand on his own two feet. He loved her too much, he told himself. He couldn't help it.

He put his hands on her shoulders, but she twisted free. "Don't, Chet."

"We'll be out of here by morning. Doesn't that make you feel better, Jane?"

"We should never have come here in the first place. You can see that now, can't you?"

"All right, yes. It was a mistake."

"You know you had no right to ask me to come here."

"We've been over that before. I told you I was sorry."

"Well, we'll talk about it when we get home," Jane said.

He hesitated. "Honey?"

She sat on the edge of the bed and studied her broken fingernail. He felt helpless. He felt angry. He wanted to slap her and make love to her, right now. He wanted to take her by force, no matter what happened. He started toward her, and someone knocked on the door.

44

Jane looked at him, startled. For a moment, fear shone in her wide gray eyes. Chet picked up the gun. "Who is it?" he called.

"M'sieu Larkin? Madame? You are safe?" It was Felix Bourges, the proprietor. "May I enter for a moment?"

"Of course," Chet said.

He shifted the gun to his left hand and tossed his own flannel robe to Jane. Then he slid back the bolts on the wooden door and opened it an inch or two. It was Bourges. The Frenchman was small and dapper in a gray seersucker suit, with a round perspiring face and a heavy moustache. His hair was very thin, showing a freckled scalp through the strands. He stood alone in the corridor. Chet let him in, and Felix entered with a sidling motion.

"*Mon Dieu,* it was a close one, no? You are certain you are all right, madame?"

Jane said, "It's a fine thing, when your guests get shot at."

"Jane, it wasn't Felix' fault," Chet said quickly.

"My apologies, madame. But the danger is ended, I think." Felix laughed and reached back into the hallway and lifted a rifle, patted it, and put it down out of sight again. "I am a member of the territorials, you know. We colonists have to fight our own battles many a time. Some of those devils actually reached the market place here, but my friends and I drove them back." His eyes lingered on Jane's body. She hadn't bothered to throw on Chet's flannel robe. Chet felt a pang of embarrassment for her and said, "Is everything all right here?"

"Oh, yes, no one was injured." Bourges sank into a rattan chair and puffed out his lips as he expelled an exhausted breath. "It is a serious matter." Felix got up and helped himself to brandy from the Martel bottle. "You two are the last of my guests."

"I've had a call from DeGrasse, by the way," Chet said. "There's a plane coming in tonight. We're flying out on it in the morning."

"Perhaps you are the fortunate ones, then. A plane, you say?" Felix swallowed the brandy. His round face was shiny with sweat. "It will be the regular mail flight from Algiers." He looked at his watch. "Due now. We can go on the roof to watch for it, if you like."

"Good," Jane said. "I could use the air."

"Is it safe?" Chet asked.

"The fighting in the town is over."

Felix was correct about the fighting in the town, but the crackle of gunfire still came from the outskirts of Marbruk as Chet and Jane stepped out on the roof of the hotel. From the crenelated parapet, Chet could see across the jumbled alleys and streets to where a fire burned luridly on some farm in the foothills. The hot wind blowing from the south made the flames leap crazily.

"The airfield is over there," Felix said, pointing.

Chet saw lights come on in the long crisscross pattern to the southwest. At the same moment he heard the drone of a single-engine plane over the town. He looked at Jane as she leaned against the parapet. She was smiling. She had not looked so happy since he had met her at Maison Blanche in Algiers. She had looked like that on the Rue Michelet, that day they went shopping. And that afternoon, in the shadowed heat of their hotel room, when they were alone. It was a lifetime ago, never to be recaptured.

He knew what Jane was thinking. The plane meant rescue for her, deliverance from heat and boredom and dirt. Freedom from him, too. He didn't want to think about it. Anger moved in him. He had yielded everything he could, including his self-respect. But he still didn't know if it would be enough for her.

The plane was landing now. He saw it distinctly, a bright yellow bug in the glare of a beacon that picked it up as it headed into the wind.

"It's awfully small," Jane said.

"The roads to the coast are blocked," Felix Bourges told her. "The telegraph lines are down. And those devils out there have a radio-jamming station that prevents reliable communication. You are lucky, madame, that we retain control of the air."

The plane had touched down. The wings rocked a little on the rough landing strip. Chet saw Jane lean eagerly over the parapet to watch. Then the plane stopped and more lights came on, making the military hangar stand out against the black of the night. It was like watching a tiny stage far away, surrounded by dark velvet.

He saw the explosion before he heard the sound. Even before the tiny plane lurched up and went over on its nose, one wing crumpling, he knew it had been a grenade, thrown by someone on the dark edge of the landing strip. He saw some people get out of the plane and stumble away. Two, then another. He couldn't be sure

46

about it, because the distance was too great. Felix began to swear in a mixture of French and Arabic. Jane made a small moaning sound.

There came another explosion, and the plane in front of the hangar burst into red and yellow flames.

Chapter Eight

DURELL felt the blast of heat from the exploding plane like the slap of a giant hand. The thought flickered through his mind that the man who had thrown it had waited just a minute too long. The pilot and Madeleine had already descended, and he had just followed them. There had been no other passengers.

A sheet of flame burst from the tanks, and he fell, grabbing at Madeleine to shield her from the heat, and then they picked themselves up and ran into the darkness at the edge of the strip. The light from the burning plane expanded, following them. The pilot was all right. There were sirens, and a racing jeep that swung toward them. Durell watched the plane burn from the edge of the field. He kept a firm grip on Madeleine's arm. The girl was shaken, but nobody was hurt. He heard the sudden rattle of an automatic rifle at the edge of the field, and the spotlight caught the running figure of a man in ragged khaki. The man screamed and twisted and fell as the rifle chattered again. Half-a-dozen French paratroopers in green berets, their weapons slung from shoulder straps, ran toward the guerrilla. The jeep swung their way, raising dust and sand in the eerie shafts of light moving over the landing strip.

"You don't have to hold me," Madeleine said. "I'm all right. And I won't run away."

Durell let her go and they walked toward the jeep. It stopped in front of them. A man in the uniform of the regular French Army jumped out and waved his driver to stay behind the wheel.

"Monsieur Durell? Mademoiselle Sardelle? Captain DeGrasse."

Durell shook hands with the Frenchman. DeGrasse was over forty, blond and hard and slender, wearing sweat-stained khaki with a string of grenades slung from one shoulder, a carbine from another. On his shirt were red captain's insignia, and among the ribbons on his breast was the black and green of the Cross of the Liberation with a number of palms, the Legion of Honor, and several from the Indo-Chinese campaign that had ended so tragically at Dien-bien-phu. There was a thin streak of blood across his jaw. He smiled ruefully. His voice was calm, deep, assured.

"My apologies. You landed in the middle of a boiling kettle, eh? The rebels surprised us again. Our plans will have to be changed, I am afraid. However, your prisoner is quite safe. How you will get him out of here is a matter we must consider with care tomorrow."

"By tomorrow I want to be back in France," Durell said.

DeGrasse shook his head. "Quite impossible, monsieur. But we can discuss the situation at ease at Felix' hotel. I am sure you will wish to rest the remainder of the night. Mademoiselle, will you please sit up front with the driver?"

Madeleine said, "How is L'Heureux, captain? Is he all right?"

"You mean is he well, in good health? Yes, the beast lives. I wish I had shot him out of hand two days ago. I have a feeling that tonight's disturbance was an effort on the part of the rebels to take our prize from us." DeGrasse took Madeleine's arm and helped her into the jeep. "We will go to the hotel first. It is quite safe now. The rebels will not attack again tonight. You can see how the situation is here, very uncertain, quite dangerous for visitors." DeGrasse smiled briefly. He had a boyish face enhanced by his rakish black beret and bright tawny eyes. "We managed to kill a round dozen of the devils tonight, at any rate."

"I would like to see L'Heureux as soon as possible," Durell said. "And I would like to talk to you in private about Orrin Boston, if I may."

"Of course. My orders are to give you every assistance. Both you and your charming aide." DeGrasse told the bearded driver to go to the Marbruk Hotel and sank back on the hard seat of the jeep. He slung his carbine around to hold it on his knees. "You will wish to refresh yourselves first."

"Just what is your situation, captain?" Durell asked. "Are we cut off from the coast here?"

"In most ways. Communication is impossible for the

48

moment. I had planned to send a military convoy with you, but I will not be able to spare the men and equipment, after tonight. Not until things settle down, at any rate."

"When do you expect that to be?"

"Two or three days, monsieur."

"Perhaps you can spare a single truck or car."

"I would not attempt the trip alone, m'sieu."

"I know the country," Durell said. "I've been here before."

"Ah, I see. During the war?"

"Yes."

"I shall give your suggestion serious consideration," DeGrasse said.

It was only a ten-minute drive from the airfield to the hotel. The streets were narrow, sometimes barely passable for the jeep, and DeGrasse kept his carbine ready, his eyes on the dark, leaning walls of the houses that loomed over them. No one moved on the streets except an occasional hurrying figure, sometimes in burnoose and robe, sometimes in European clothing. At frequent intervals they passed patrols of territorials or regular armed troopers on guard.

The bearded French jeep driver escorted Madeleine into the lobby, carrying the small piece of luggage she had salvaged from the plane. Durell halted DeGrasse on the silent terrace under the lights.

"Could you spare a man or two for the next hour?" he asked quietly. "I would like to have the girl guarded."

DeGrasse looked mildly surprised. "But she is your associate, monsieur."

"Not exactly," Durell said. "She is suspect. I'll explain later. But it is important that she be prevented from making any local contacts without my presence."

"You will return here for the night, however?"

"I'd like to see Orrin Boston's room first—the place where he lived—and look it over. Then I'll want to talk to L'Heureux."

DeGrasse's face clouded. "I will be glad to get rid of that one. I was fond of Orrin Boston, you know. He knew this country and the people, and he was of great assistance to me in the matter of maintaining contact with the local population. His death was a tragedy that never should have happened."

"What do you know about it?"

49

DeGrasse shrugged. His youthful face looked tired in the harsh glare of light from the open doors of the hotel. "L'Heureux shot him twice, once in the lung and once more in the stomach. Monsieur Boston was dead when we found him."

"And where was that?"

"In the south quarter of the town. It is my belief that Boston was negotiating with dissident elements among the rebels. He would not tell me what the subject of his negotiations was, but for the last week he was very cheerful and optimistic. He seemed to expect great things from his work as mediator."

"Did he mention any particular sums of money being involved?"

DeGrasse looked puzzled. "No, monsieur."

"Did he tell you any of his thoughts about L'Heureux?"

DeGrasse rubbed his smooth jaw. "I distrusted L'Heureux, you know. This American had an undesirable reputation, you understand. But I had to be tactful. Boston said he knew all about the man and was on his guard and chose to employ him in his negotiations with the rebels. But evidently Boston was not careful enough, eh?"

"Why are you so sure L'Heureux killed him?"

"He was caught on the spot by the locals. It was in Orrin Boston's flat, behind a Moslem café run by a Kabyle who was friendly with Boston. When they heard the shots they rushed in and found Boston dying and L'Heureux with the gun in his hand. L'Heureux tried to maintain it was a terrorist murder, but no one else was on the scene. He is guilty, monsieur. And I do not envy your job of taking him back to the frustrating processes of justice." DeGrasse slapped his carbine. "Orrin Boston was a man highly respected by everyone here. Even loved, one might say. My own brand of justice for his murder would be cleaner and quicker."

"My orders are to bring L'Heureux back unharmed," Durell said.

"And mine are to assist you in every possible way."

"Then I shall want a truck and a driver by tomorrow morning."

"The nearest contact with other Army units who could give you reliable escort to Algiers is well over a hundred kilometers to the north. I could not spare an escort large enough to insure your safety. Not for several days, at any rate."

"No escort at all would be better than one that is too small, yet attracts attention. Do you understand?"

"We shall discuss it at your convenience."

"Now, if I may see Orrin Boston's living quarters," Durell suggested quietly.

The jeep driver, who said his name was Jean Letou, was a sweaty man in a stained uniform, steel-helmeted, with tired, bloodshot eyes that peered with suspicion at every shadow on the narrow, twisting streets they followed. Durell carried a snub-nosed .38, but he kept it in his pocket. He had to remember this was not his war.

The town was quiet. Durell looked at his watch and saw it was almost midnight. Here and there a hurrying figure showed briefly in the shadows, and the driver tensed physically as they passed by, but nothing happened. They were moving away from the sector of town where the raid had occurred. Jean turned down a narrow street where the stone houses seemed to lean over them, their balconies almost touching overhead to form a tunnel. Lights shone ahead in a small square. Garish, naked bulbs gleamed over a long, high wall where someone had daubed in red paint, *A bas les francaises!* The driver made a spitting sound in his beard as they lurched by and then halted the jeep in front of the dim entrance to a café.

"I had better go in with you, monsieur. It is difficult to guess how they will regard a stranger. They are always nervous after the rebel attack. Afraid of their brothers and afraid of the settlers' territorial squads who make reprisals."

Durell surveyed the shadowy native building and the surrounding alleys. "Did Boston live here?"

"He lived everywhere, they say, but this was his headquarters."

"Were these people his friends?"

"Everyone was his friend, monsieur."

Durell looked at him. "Except for one."

"*Merde.*" The driver spit again, wiped his beard with a thick hand, and took his carbine and stood on the rough sidewalk. "We have that one locked up at the command post. It is a disappointment he will not be shot. I myself volunteered for the firing squad."

"Let's go in," Durell said.

The thin wail of a flute and the rhythmic beat of a

51

goatskin drum came from inside the café. There were several wooden tables inside and half-a-dozen Moslems in European dress drinking tea. The music, Durell saw, came from a radio. A dark-faced girl in a gray skirt and pink blouse came toward them smiling, and then she stopped smiling.

"Jean, everything is quiet here," she said quickly to the jeep driver. "There has been no trouble at all."

"It is this man," Jean said, waving to Durell. "He has come for Monsieur Boston's belongings."

Someone turned off the radio and the music stopped. There was silence in the small, smoky room. Two of the Arabs got up and walked out. The girl looked at Durell with sullen, hostile eyes. "There is nothing to take. He owned very little, wanted very little."

"I'd like to look around, anyway," Durell said.

"As you wish, m'sieu. Follow me."

She led the way through an arched doorway in the back of the room and out through a heavy wooden gate into a back garden. The change in atmosphere was startling, after the squalid café. A small fountain tinkled with gentle splashings. A flight of stone steps scaled the outside wall ahead to a doorway on a balcony above.

The bearded French driver said, "You go first, Zorah."

The Arab girl smiled scornfully. "The rebels are not here. There is no trap. There is no need to be afraid."

"Nevertheless, you go first."

She shrugged and climbed the outside steps to the door and opened it. When she had put on a light, Durell followed the soldier in and closed the door behind him.

There was a heavy baroque desk that looked incongruous amid the delicately wrought Arab pieces. Durell went to it and opened several of the drawers. The papers inside had been pawed around hurriedly. He looked in a scented wardrobe closet. The fragments of a smashed radio tube glittered in brittle silver slivers on the floor inside. That was all.

"Captain DeGrasse went through everything, m'sieu," Zorah offered. She stood near the doorway, her arms folded across her breasts, one hip askew. "There was nothing of importance here, I heard him say."

Durell nodded and went to the window and looked out at the courtyard they had entered. Darkness ruled down there. He couldn't see anything. He returned to the wardrobe and looked at Orrin Boston's European

clothing and the fine Arab *kachabia* he must have worn
often. Durell's eyes were dark and brooding. Boston had
loved this Moslem world, and he had been doing a good
job for K Section here.

He turned to the girl. "You were here the night he
was killed?"

"Not here. Downstairs, entertaining."

"Do you work in the café regularly?"

"Yes. I also cooked for Monsieur Boston and did his
laundry."

"You were fond of him?"

The girl's eyes were large and dark. "I loved him,
m'sieu."

Durell was relentless. "How much did you love him?"

"We were—I did everything I could for him. All that
he permitted and accepted. I knew about his wife and
family. I think he loved them and loved me, too. He was
a deeply troubled man in that respect, living in two
worlds, yet drifting as one lost on the sea."

"Who killed him?"

"It was Charles L'Heureux," she said flatly.

"Did you see it happen?"

"I was one of the first to run up here when we heard
the shot in the café. They had been quarreling, and
finally they began to fight. We heard the sounds of the
struggle and then the shot. It was over very quickly,
m'sieu."

"And L'Heureux was in this room when you came in?"

"Yes. With the gun in his hand."

"Did he admit killing Orrin Boston?"

"He is a devil, that one. A laughing devil. At first he
tried to say it was a terrorist. But we know no one was
here from the rebels. I—I tried to kill him." She lifted
her skirt and showed a long, thin poniard strapped to
her firm thigh. "With this, m'sieu. But he is strong, that
one. He laughed and took it away from me. Then the
soldiers arrived and they took him away. And the body."
She made a dim swallowing sound and her face twisted
with grief. "Orrin is buried in the military cemetery at the
command post."

Durell looked around the ornate Moorish room again.
He wondered who had taken Orrie's radio. He tried to
feel the presence of the man who had lived here, to
capture the sight and sound and look of him, but it
was difficult to place him in this alien environment.

53

Nobody had mentioned the huge sum of American currency that had vanished. He decided not to say anything about it, either. He looked at the French jeep driver. "Let's go, Jean."

The bearded soldier turned his bulky form toward the door and waved his carbine at the Arab girl. "Forward, *petite*."

"Don't push me," she said. "I live here."

"This place is restricted," the soldier said. "Go first."

The girl looked resentful as she went out. The courtyard below was filled with shadows that moved in the wind and the moonlight. Durell closed the door and descended the stone stairway outside. The girl slipped ahead through the gateway to the garden behind the café, and then the jeep driver followed.

Durell did not see it happen. He came through the gateway in time to hear the thud of the thrown knife as it landed in the soldier's back. He heard the grunt forced from the bearded man's open mouth, then the crash as the soldier fell. Durell dropped to one knee and crouched in the shadows against the high, vine-grown wall. The Arab girl had turned at the sound. She was beyond the fountain, on the other side of the garden, near the back door to the café. She screamed.

Durell's gun was in his hand. He felt hard stones under his knee, he saw the shadows moving intangibly against the walls of the dark, silent houses around them. The man with the knife could be anywhere. He looked briefly at Jean. The soldier was dead. The knife had been thrown with deadly aim. Its hilt shone with polished wood and that part of the blade extruding from the Frenchman's back glistened in the moonlight.

The Arab girl screamed again. Durell felt the fury of frustration. The ambusher was too well concealed. He wasn't moving to betray his position. There was nothing to shoot at.

Then there came a shout from the house to his left, and a muffled shot. A whistle blew, high and shrill, from the street beyond the café entrance. Another shot cracked. Durell stepped over the dead man and ran through the café to the street. The Arabs in the café sat frozen at their tables. Their dark faces were like stone.

In the street, a French patrol was fanning out toward the nearest corner. A man stood on one of the high roofs there, holding a rifle. One of the troopers took aim

54

and fired carefully. The man was a dark shadow, rigid for a moment against the moonlit sky. Then he fell, cartwheeling to the street three floors below. His body made an ugly breaking sound as he hit. The French soldier who had fired the shot got up and walked toward the body and kicked it futilely.

"He was a sniper the rebels left behind," a young lieutenant said breathlessly. "Was anyone hurt?"

"One of your comrades lies behind the café with a knife in his back," Durell said.

"Your driver?"

"Yes."

"These murderers grow more fanatic every day. I knew Jean well." The lieutenant sent two men hurrying through the café. Durell looked for the Arab girl, but he didn't see her. He pocketed his gun. The young lieutenant was staring at him. The Frenchman said, "You will need another man to escort you back to the hotel."

"I'm not going back to the hotel just yet," Durell said.

The command post in the farmhouse was only a short drive from town. Durell took the jeep there himself. The sentries waved him past the barbed wire into the compound, which was floodlighted by powerful spots placed on steel posts. Durell noted the weary anger and tension on the faces of the troops.

DeGrasse was in his office. He still wore his black beret, but he had unslung the set of grenades dangling from his shoulders. He looked exhausted. He listened to what Durell told him about the murder and nodded. "Another one, then. It is often this way. For no reason, a good man dies. I shall have to write to his wife."

"And the assassin?"

"He was also a man. And dead, too. One wonders, monsieur, where the balance lies."

DeGrasse agreed to let him talk to L'Heureux alone. Durell followed a guard to the big barn across the compound and walked up the steps to what had been the loft, now divided into cells. The soldier unlocked the heavy wooden door and stepped back with his rifle ready, speaking to the man inside. "You have a visitor, pig."

Durell went in. The guard outside snapped on a light and Charles L'Heureux sat up slowly on the cot. He grinned at Durell.

"Well, chum. All the way from Washington?"

"I've come to take you back with me," Durell said.

"You got an American cigarette?" L'Heureux asked casually. "I'm all out."

Durell tossed a pack to the prisoner in silence. He took in L'Heureux' massive frame, the aura of arrogance, the blond hair and black brows, the feeling of strength and brutality in him. L'Heureux lit the cigarette gratefully and turned his back on Durell to look out through the tiny cell window. "Is the raid over?"

"Just about," Durell said.

"Many casualties?"

"Some. Even one is too many."

"Was that your plane that burned?"

"Yes."

"So how do we get out of this trap?" L'Heureux turned back to Durell again. His eyes were dark and mocking and intelligent. "You say you came to take me back. Is it for a trial?"

"For murdering Orrie Boston."

L'Heureux looked down at his cigarette.

Durell said, "You don't deny killing him, do you?"

"No."

"How did it happen?"

L'Heureux looked bland. "It was self-defense, chum."

"Do you expect us to believe that?"

"I've got plenty to tell," L'Heureux said sharply. His words betrayed a trace of down-East twang. He sounded angry. "That's the real reason they sent you for me, isn't it? To pump me dry, then shoot me."

"That depends on what you have to say."

"Listen, I guess you knew Orrie, right? Or you thought you did. Maybe you worked with him back in the States. All right. A great guy, huh? And I'm the rat that put a slug in him. That's the picture, right?"

"Can you change it?" Durell asked.

"I don't give a damn what you and your desk jockeys think. I didn't ask for the job. I was doing all right here. I had my business to take care of."

"What kind of business?" Durell asked.

"Import and export," L'Heureux said, grinning again.

"Running guns?"

"Nobody complained, see? Anyway, Orrie invited me to work for him and I did. A patriotic duty, he said. Humanitarian work, to help end this war, he said." Irony

56

ran through the prisoner's words like a dark, scarlet thread. "So this is what I get for it. Listen, *I* knew what Orrie was doing. I knew all about that Arab girl he slept with. He was gettin' information from her about the rebels. He was funneling dough to the rebels, did you know that? Playing hand in glove with them. He'd sold out to the Reds who are backing them."

"That kind of lying won't buy anything," Durell said. He was aware of anger. "Orrin Boston wasn't a Red. And the Communists have little or no control over the rebel."

"No, but they'd like to get in. They offer all the war equipment they need, in exchange for running the show. You know what would happen then. And Orrie was helping them get a foot in the door. Look, I caught Orrie with some of the guerrilla leaders. I hung him up on it. The rebels got away that night, and Orrie and I went up to his apartment to talk it out. He had a lot of cash in that place, but it wasn't there when we got there. He gave it to the rebels." L'Heureux looked at Durell with cool, pale eyes. "What Orrie meant to do up there was to kill me to shut me up. And when he pulled the gun, I jumped him."

Durell listened to the man's smooth, quick words. They were lies. Clever, assured lies. He knew Orrin Boston better than to believe any of it.

L'Heureux laughed softly. "Orrie was too old for that hot little Arab playmate of his. Zorah made him into a dried-out old man. So I got the gun from him and it went off. I didn't want to kill him. Just put him under arrest and turn him over to you people and go back to my own business. But he got killed and the Frenchies here were all set to line me up against the wall for knockin' off their phony tin god. Maybe you want to do it, too. Well, it's no skin off my nose, believe me. You can think what you like. But I ain't going back with you."

"Do you have a choice?" Durell asked.

"You won't take me back for any phony trial."

"We're starting tonight," Durell said quietly.

L'Heureux looked surprised. "Are you nuts? Your plane was wrecked."

"We'll use the roads and go by truck."

"With the country alive with the rebels tonight?"

"I think we'll make it," Durell said.

L'Heureux crushed out his cigarette on the floor. He drew a deep breath and looked at Durell and looked down at his hands. "Not with me, you won't. I'm not that crazy. I won't go."

"You'll go if it has to be in handcuffs."

"But I wouldn't have a chance—"

"That's your lookout," Durell said. "Personally, I'm sorry DeGrasse didn't shoot you out of hand. And I wouldn't care if the rebels had gotten you, either. But my orders are to take you back to Paris and then to Washington, and that's where we're going."

L'Heureux said quietly, "You'll never make it, chum. You'll be dead by morning. And I'll get away, believe me."

"You can try," Durell said. "You're welcome to try."

He waited a moment. The prisoner's story was brash and arrogant, and Durell wondered at his inner confidence. He didn't know how much truth and how many clever lies went into the concoction L'Heureux spun about Orrin Boston's death. The man wouldn't be easy to break. He could stick to his story indefinitely, proclaiming his innocence through weeks of questioning. It was not Durell's job to do this. His job was to bring the man in.

He turned to go, and L'Heureux stopped him with a gesture. The man suddenly looked uncomfortable and uncertain. "Just one thing, friend. It's kind of important to me."

"Yes?"

"Did Madeleine Sardelle tell you people about me?"

"Why?"

"I'd kind of like to know. She's my girl. I know she's with those French cops, working for that guy Brumont. She told me all about that. She'll tell you I never killed anybody. Not like murder, I mean."

"Don't count on any help from her," Durell said.

"Look, did she come here with you?"

"What if she did?" Durell asked carefully.

"I'd like to see her. Talk to her."

Durell watched the prisoner's face for any telltale sign of satisfaction in the knowledge that Madeleine was in Marbruk. But the man gave nothing away. His face expressed concern only.

"You're not going to take her with us tonight, are you?" L'Heureux asked. "This is no country for a girl. And she's got nothing to do with what you charge me with, anyway. You can't take her by truck to the coast tonight.

First place, we won't make it. And if you try, we're all likely to be killed before we get ten kilometers out of town."

"She'll come along with us," Durell said flatly.

He kept watching L'Heureux, but he couldn't tell if this was what the man wanted to hear. He left the cell a moment later.

Chapter Nine

MADELEINE undressed slowly, almost languidly, and ran water into the bath next to her room in the Marbruk Hotel. She had bolted the heavy door in the face of the curious guard posted in the corridor outside. Now she listened for any more of the sporadic gunfire on the edge of town, but it seemed quiet enough now. The raid was over.

She heard several sharp, isolated rifle shots, and she shivered in spite of the steamy heat of the bath. No need to be afraid, though. Durell was competent, of course, but Charley would take care of him. After she prepared the way, that is.

She lifted her breasts with her hands, studying the still-smooth, firm lines of her body with critical eyes. She bathed quickly, then changed into a dark skirt and white blouse chosen from the single piece of luggage she had taken with her.

When she had combed her long red hair and put on fresh lipstick, she walked barefooted to the bedroom door and opened it.

The soldier on guard in the corridor grinned at her. "Something, mademoiselle?"

"Has Monsieur Durell returned yet?"

"No, mademoiselle."

"May I wait for him in his room?"

"It would be irregular."

"But I feel so nervous. His room is next to mine, isn't it?" She smiled warmly at the man. He was really only a boy, torn from his job and family in France by the Army draft. "If I could unlock the connecting door."

"I have no key."

"It must be in the door on his side. Please? It is only a small favor."

59

The guard was a Frenchman, after all. He stood up, holding his carbine easily in his left hand. "Go into your room, mademoiselle, and wait one moment."

She smiled warmly when the Frenchman finally unlocked the connecting door. He looked as if he wanted to linger, but thought better of it.

"Thank you a thousand times," she said.

"It is nothing, mademoiselle."

She did not go into Durell's room immediately. She tested the door to make sure she really had access to his quarters, then went to the telephone and lifted it, pleased to hear the buzzing that indicated the raiders hadn't destroyed local communications, at any rate. A man's voice asked for her number and she gave one she had committed to memory some time ago. The military was running the telephone system, she knew, and for a moment the sense of danger, if her call was monitored, made her lower the phone and almost replace it on the hook. Then she lifted it to her ear again and spoke in Arabic.

"Sidi Gamal?" she asked quietly.

"Who wishes to speak to him?"

"An old friend who has just arrived. I am sure he knows about my arrival."

"One minute, please."

She waited. She had kept her voice low, in order not to alert the interest of the guard outside. The town was very quiet now. There was no more shooting anywhere. A truckload of territorials went through the market place below, and she heard the clinking of arms and the creak of leather and an occasional sulphurous curse.

"Mademoiselle?"

She turned back to the telephone. "I am home."

"Good. Then you received my message. All is well?"

"As well as one might expect. And our friend?"

"Unable to move."

"He is to be moved soon," Mademoiselle said. "I am here to help."

"Plans have been made. But they are tentative. One does not know the time or method of removal."

"I will inform you," she said, "when I learn it myself."

"Good. Keep yourself safe. Peace be with you."

"And to you, peace," Madeleine said, returning the formula.

She hung up. Sidi Gamal, in his hideout, wherever

it was, would alert the rebels to help Charley get free. She had made contact. Now it was only a matter of time and persuasion. Her spirits lifted. Time would pass, and Durell would return. She could persuade him. She had confidence in her body to move any man. Once she knew Durell's plans, it would be simple.

She looked at her watch. It was almost midnight. It had been a long, tiring day. Paris, and the rain, and Madame Sofie's salon belonged to another world, another time. It was hard to realize she had come so far so fast. Madame Sofie's might never have existed.

Then she remembered the men who had tried to kidnap her in Paris, and a little shiver of fear touched her. She was afraid because she did not understand. The men were not of the National Liberation Front. She was sure of that. And she could not figure out who they were or why they had attacked her.

She told herself to forget it. Nothing serious had happened, anyway. She went into Durell's room and stood looking at his bed, as she had looked at many beds before. The dim light from her own room followed her and cast a slab of yellow across the tiled floor. The light touched a corner of the tall, narrow window on the balcony that overlooked the market place. The hotel was quiet. She touched Durell's suitcase with her bare toe. The leather felt warm against her skin. She tried the latch, but the suitcase was locked, and she was not too interested in opening it and searching within. Her methods were different.

She loosened the catch on her skirt and let it rustle softly down her hips and thighs in a heap to the floor, and then she stepped out of it. She took off her blouse, shook her red hair loose again, and sat down naked on Durell's bed to wait for him. She felt supremely confident that he would not reject what she had to offer.

A few minutes went by. Madeleine relaxed on the bed, feeling the heat of the North African night like a thick blanket over her naked body. She heard a sound from the young guard in the corridor, then the tinny cacophony of radio music from somewhere in the hotel, then a man's voice, oddly distorted, speaking in Arabic in a vituperative harangue against the French. Madeleine wished whoever was listening to the propaganda would turn it off. She didn't care about it, one way or another. If all went well, she would soon be far away.

61

But the volume of the radio seemed to come louder, beating against her quiet, wishful thoughts. Through the shrill screaming of propaganda she heard a small thudding noise from the guard's position in the corridor beyond the door. She sat up, leaning on one elbow in the semidarkness. She thought Durell might be returning, and this started a quickening sensation in her that surprised her, because a man was nothing new to her, and what she planned to do was no novelty. Yet she thought it might be different with this one. She didn't know why. Perhaps because she recognized the danger in him.

The door opened and a man came in. The door was closed.

"Mademoiselle."

It was not Durell's voice.

The man was a tall shadow in a native robe. She could see only the angularity of a narrow face when he turned toward her. And then she caught the glimmer of a steel knife in his hand.

"Go back to your room, mademoiselle, and be silent."

She sat up. Her nakedness did not trouble her. But it did not interest the intruder, either.

"Who are you?" she whispered.

She saw his movement as a sliding shadow when he bolted the door. The lock clicked. When he came toward her, her fear mounted. She suddenly remembered the men in Paris. There were too many factions in the rebel movement, fighting one another. Had Charley angered one, betrayed one group to gain the favor of another? She opened her mouth to scream, and his reaction came with the speed of a striking snake. His hand clapped over her mouth and his fingers pinched her nostrils shut. She couldn't breathe.

All at once panic took her beyond control. She tried to drag the strangling hand from her mouth, but the man's fingers were like ropes of steel. She lurched to her feet, striking, kicking. There was an odor to the man that urged further terror in her. Her brain screamed at him to let her go. There was a roaring in her ears and she knew she could not break free. A great wave of despair broke darkly over her. She stopped fighting. She let her weight grow suddenly limp.

Her collapse took the man by surprise. He released her, and she slumped to the floor.

The last thing she remembered was his rough hands violating her body, picking her up with ease and carrying her off somewhere into welcome darkness. . . .

Durell returned to the hotel ten minutes later and found the guard sprawled in the corridor in front of his door. He had left Felix, the manager, down in the lobby locking up the hotel. The fat proprietor had told him that DeGrasse had phoned and wanted him to call the command post again, at once.

It was quiet in the hallway. Durell knew that an American couple occupied the room farthest from the stairway. He didn't touch the young soldier once he saw that the man had been slugged and wasn't dead. He wondered what DeGrasse wanted from him that was so urgent. In the jeep, just before leaving the prison where he had talked to L'Heureux, DeGrasse had asked if it would be possible to take the Larkins to the coast with him if they were willing to risk the trip. Durell had not committed himself. He looked at the Larkins' door as he stood beside the unconscious guard. There was no sound in the hotel except a muted radio from the kitchen area below, spewing forth propaganda from Cairo.

He listened to the rasp of the soldier's irregular breathing and turned slowly. He took his gun from his pocket and walked quietly to his door, then paused. Madeleine's door, next to his, was shut and the guard had been assigned to keep an eye on her. He turned to the girl's room instead of his own.

This door was not locked. He eased it open and moved in behind the swinging panel, his gun held low so it could not be taken from him by surprise. Nothing happened. A lamp shone dimly beside the empty bed. The girl wasn't here. His eye quickly noted the connecting door that stood ajar to his room. There was nothing but silence and darkness beyond. He moved that way in silence and stood against the wall beside the door, listening.

He heard the sound of quick, frightened breathing. He decided that would be Madeleine. Then he heard a man's soft, controlled sigh. He tried to estimate how far the man was standing from the connecting door. Not more than three or four feet, he decided. Durell went in.

It was easy, after all. The shadowy figure of a man

63

was facing the opposite way, tensely watching the corridor door. Madeleine was on his bed, the coarse sheet held around her. He saw her skirt and blouse in a soft heap on the floor. He wasted no time wondering about it. He held the gun ready and spoke in Arabic, "If you are waiting for me, I am here. Drop your knife."

The man turned. In the dim light, his face was like that of an angry hawk. He dropped the poniard. It made a sharp clattering sound on the tiled floor.

"I come in peace," he said.

"With a knife?"

"Are you Monsieur Durell?"

"I am."

"Then I have come for you, m'sieu."

"To kill me? Why?"

"Not to kill you. I have orders to take you to a conference."

"With whom?"

The man's eyes were pale crescents sliding toward Madeleine as she sat on the bed. The girl was rubbing her throat and mouth with one hand. She held the sheet around her body with the other. "It would be best if we discussed this privately. An old friend of yours has learned of your arrival in Marbruk. He is anxious to talk to you."

"News travels fast in Marbruk."

"Events match the pace of the news, like two running camels." The man's voice was sardonic. "You do not need the gun, m'sieu."

"But you came prepared for violence."

"Only because it is necessary that you agree to come on our terms. You must come with me blindfolded and give your word you will not attempt to discover where I take you."

"I have nothing to discuss. Suppose I say no?"

"It will be to your advantage. It concerns your prisoner."

Madeleine's whisper was harsh. "Charley?"

Durell looked at her. Her face was dim and lovely, but it was also traced with uninhibited savagery in the dim light. "Go back to your room, Madeleine," he said quietly. "It would be best."

"She was in here waiting for you," said the Arab. "This harlot, this traitor."

"Go on, Madeleine," Durell said.

The girl slid off the bed and stood up. Her body looked soft and rounded as she walked past him into the other room. Durell scooped up her skirt and blouse and tossed them through the doorway after her, then closed the door and turned the key in the lock. "Stay here," he told the Arab.

He went into the corridor. The French soldier was stirring on the tiled floor beyond the threshold. His eyes held a dazed, wild look. Durell went to Madeleine's corridor door and locked that and pocketed the key. The Arab stepped into the hallway across the guard's body.

Durell said, "Who wishes to speak to me?"

"It is the Hadji, my commander. El-Abri."

"Does he remember me?"

"He remembers you with friendship, m'sieu."

"How can I be sure you're telling the truth?"

"He said to remind you of a favorite quotation of his, which he is sure you will remember. It is this: In this life, one must either be the anvil or the hammer. The strong man tries to be the hammer."

"I'll go," Durell said.

Chapter Ten

THEY LEFT the hotel by a back door. The lobby was empty and there was no sign of Felix. The Arab led the way for a few hundred yards, through one alley and then another, each redolent with smells. The moon provided the only light. Durell kept his gun in hand until they came to a small, battered Renault 4-C, a Quatre Chevaux model, parked in a courtyard. Tramping feet came to them from the opening of a crooked street nearby, and they stood in silent darkness until a U.T. patrol passed. The Arab took out a long scarf while he listened.

"The territorial units fight terror with terror. It is like a darkness on the land. You agree to be blindfolded?"

"How far must we go?"

"It will take no more than fifteen minutes, if we are not stopped by patrols."

"The Hadji is reckless to make his headquarters so close to the French."

"One can hide in the nest of the adder better than on the open rock. You may keep your gun, m'sieu. You have el-Abri's word that you will be returned safely in one hour."

The trip was no longer than the Arab said it would be. Durell tried to mark the twists and turns of the Renault's course, listening to the changing sound of the tires as they rumbled over stone, asphalt, and finally a gravelly roadway. Once they stopped abruptly, and he heard a truck lumber along not far away, and he assumed it was another U.T. patrol. He heard French voices, and then the truck went on; after a moment the Renault proceeded again, turning left, then bumping over a wooden bridge, to judge by the hollow rumbling under the wheels. Then they stopped abruptly.

"We are here, m'sieu. You may remove the blind-fold."

For a moment Durell felt a confusion of time, as if the fifteen years since his last assignment in the OSS had never been. For two months he had worked in the desert with el-Abri, who then had not yet made his pilgrimage to Mecca to earn his title of Hadji. They had been operating a radio unit then, exploring the sentiment of Arab and French settler alike, preparing for the North African invasion. He had lived in the desert as just another Berber with el-Abri, had risked capture by a Nazi counterintelligence unit, had avoided Rommel in a long swing through the deserts of Tunisia. They were both younger and wilder in those days, Durell remembered. And the postwar years had seen too many changes in this country to expect things to have remained as they had been.

When he stepped from the Renault, he saw the huddle of a *douar*, a native village of about eight *mechtas*, the mud-walled Arab houses. There were a few straggling date palms and the high, windy pressure of the mountain slopes to the north. He looked back and saw that the road they had followed twisted along the edge of a rocky wadi. An armed guard in ragged khaki lowered his rifle and nodded to the Arab and Durell.

"The Hadji is waiting. Is the American armed?"

"Yes," Durell said.

"Ah, you speak our tongue." The guard moved closer. "One does not know how the years will change a man, the Hadji says. He remembers you as a man of courage

66

and honor. But a long time has passed since he saw you last."

"The knife cuts both ways," Durell said. "I keep my gun."

"As you say."

Durell stepped into the largest of the *mechtas*. El-Abri got up from a chair behind a wooden table, where maps had been spread in apparent disarray. Durell remembered him at once. He was gray now, where he had been dark and wild and unkempt. And there was a veneer of culture over the tall Berber that hadn't been there fifteen years ago.

"Durell." His hand was hard and lean. "It is good to see you again."

"And good to see you, too," Durell said.

El-Abri smiled. "We could have enjoyed our reunion under happier circumstances, I fear. For me, it would be better if I were no longer a renegade guerrilla chief, hiding in my own land. For you and your people, the world has turned upside down, has it not? You Americans no longer walk the world in pride and arrogance."

"Humility can have a cleansing effect," Durell said.

"Would you like a drink? For myself, of course—"

"No, thank you. You asked to see me, Hadji, but not in friendship. Only in a state of truce."

"We have no quarrel, you and I. Please sit down. Forgive me if you think I greet you with a taunt and a jeering phrase. But what I said is true, is it not? Between East and West, the balance has tipped against you. You no longer have the comfort of complacency. The world walks on the edge of a knife."

"We can use that knife to pare some of our fat," Durell said. "We respect our rivals now, and that is good."

He sat down. "Your war with the French is not my war, and I am not permitted to take part in it or even to venture an opinion on it. If I am here under terms of truce, then I must warn you not to tell me anything I should not know. I may be considered a neutral, yet most of my associations are with the French. Do you understand?"

El-Abri smiled. "You are here as a friend, then, unless you choose otherwise."

"Agreed."

"You look well."

"And you, too."

"Much time has passed since our old victory, Durell."

"The war is not yet over," Durell said.

There was a single, smoky kerosene lantern in the one-room hut, and the Berber chieftain turned it up slightly so that its yellow light flared out in the bare room. His teeth gleamed whitely as he smiled. His face was the face of the desert, lean and dry, scarred under a thin gray beard. He wore a khaki uniform, the trousers stuffed into American paratrooper's boots. El-Abri was armed with a German Schmeiser and a long, wicked-looking knife in a leather scabbard. His pale brown eyes were brooding and intelligent.

"Did you know I spent four years in Paris after the liberation?" the Berber asked abruptly. "I learned the ways of the French and then I went to Mecca and then I attended the Arabic University of Zitouna, in Tunis. By that time the resistance movement was in full swing and I joined it. Your war has not ended, and indeed, is going badly for you, Durell. My war is the same. But today we fight, if not on opposite sides, at least in different directions."

"I wish it were otherwise," Durell said.

"But you and I are not enemies, and never will be."

"Let's hope not."

El-Abri sighed. "Yet the fighting will go on. The relationship between Arab and Frenchman must not be that of horse and rider."

"You don't hate the French, then," Durell said.

"No. I hate the extremists of both parties, if you must know. The French territorials, the settlers, the proprietors call us gooks and want to continue the attitude of treating us as inferior people, using terror and violence to prolong the war between us, just as much as the rebel factions have now become intransigent and refuse to treat or negotiate."

"You didn't send for me, though, to give me a political lecture," Durell said.

"You wonder why I sent for you. The French would like to know about this *douar*. I should tell you, first, that tonight's raid on Marbruk was not my operation. It was the extremist faction."

"You don't work together?"

Something flickered in the Kabyle's tawny eyes. "No. It has not been so for some time. This is my territory and my people live here, and I have been in command since the fighting began. But recently the extremists came in and demanded jurisdiction. Until then, I managed to keep things peaceful. There was no terror, no murders." El-Abri's eyes darkened. "Unlike the extremists, I refuse to kill Arabs who remain loyal to the French. We owe much to France and will owe more before our legitimate aims are achieved. And long afterward, as well."

"You do not speak like a man of violence," Durell said.

"I have had enough of it."

"But you bear arms and command troops."

"A great many *harkas*, or units. Yes. I only wish what will be best for my people and Algeria. One moves with the winds of the desert. Or one dies. I shall be truthful with you, Durell. As an old comrade, you will understand. I know why you are here. I knew you were coming before you left Paris. Our intelligence is very, very good. I knew your friend, Orrin Boston. He was my friend, too. We talked often about you. I have said prayers for him since his death."

"Was Orrie negotiating with you?"

"Yes."

"For a truce?" Durell asked tentatively.

El-Abri smiled thinly. It was like a movement in granite. "You are an astute man. I trusted Orrin Boston. Yes, I was negotiating for a truce with the French. After the extremists came in, I searched my conscience for the right and wrong of this war. The extremists use violence, murder, looting. They think they can win the rebellion this way and hope for stability afterward. I believe otherwise. I believe in negotiation to achieve Algerian aims. For this reason—and because your enemies, too, seek to blow up the sands of the Sahara to obscure their own aims against you—I was prepared to surrender with my two thousand men to the French."

Durell sat back in the hard wooden chair. Nothing changed in his face, but he knew the importance of el-Abri's announcement. Few of the rebels had dared to surrender, in view of the extremist terror behind them. If a truce here could be achieved, a chain reaction might result that could bring reason and eventual peace in a reasonable time. He understood now what Orrin Boston was trying to do. Peace anywhere in the world was worth any effort, and desirable for the West.

"What stopped your plans to surrender, then?" Durell asked. "You haven't laid down your arms, Hadji."

The Berber said flatly, "Because I was betrayed."

"Not by Orrin Boston," Durell said.

"No, no. By his assistant, that man L'Heureux. The man you claim as your prisoner." The Kabyle's eyes were like hard topaz as he leaned forward into the light of the kerosene lamp. "Listen and understand, Durell. You think it will perhaps be a small thing if I surrender with my small force of men. Maybe so. A small event in a large and troubled world. But who knows which straw, Durell, will tip the scales for or against the Western world?"

Durell nodded. "Hadji, you know me of old. If I fight for anything, it is to see men live in peace, through reason, not locked in a struggle to kill each other."

"Yes, you were always like that," el-Abri mused. "Well, I was prepared to surrender, granted amnesty. It was all arranged by Orrin Boston, and Captain DeGrasse knew my intentions. But I was betrayed, as I said. As I took my men down out of the mountains, I marched them unwittingly into an ambush. The ambush was not made by the French. It was sprung by my so-called brothers of the extremists. Someone informed them of my readiness to negotiate, and because of their fanaticism and zeal, they set a trap for me. It was a massacre, my friend. Many of my men fell."

"But you escaped," Durell said quietly.

"Yes. And we took one of the extremists a prisoner. We made him talk. It was not easy. Nothing is easy in the desert. The prisoner was a lieutenant, and I had to torture him before his tongue loosened. He told me that your agent, Charles L'Heureux, working for Orrin Boston, tipped his commanders that I was coming out of the mountains to negotiate a surrender. So they waited for me and tried to wipe us out. They failed. And now I know that L'Heureux killed your friend and mine, Orrin Boston, when Boston learned of L'Heureux' part in the affair. The blood of many of my men are on this man's hands. And he is the man you have come to take back with you as a prisoner."

Durell nodded. From outside the hut came the measured tread of a guard's boots on the rocky shale at the edge of the *wadi*. The wind had changed. The chill of a desert night was in the air.

"What are your plans now, Hadji?" he asked.

"I still wish to surrender. I believe my way is right."

"And what about your men?"

"They will follow me. They are lonely for their women and their own *mechtas*. We have discussed it democratically. They will go where I lead them."

"I can arrange it for you," Durell said. "Perhaps I can finish Orrin Boston's work."

"That would be fitting," el-Abri said. "But there is a condition." The Kabyle's thin face was harsh. "The condition is L'Heureux. You must give him to me. And then I will surrender to DeGrasse."

"No," Durell said.

"It is a small thing. Perhaps you do not yet understand. He caused many good men to die because of his greed and treachery. And he killed Orrin Boston."

"What would you do with him?"

"I intend to kill him."

"I'm sorry," Durell said. "You can't have L'Heureux."

The guerrilla commander stood up and walked to the door of the hut and looked out at the desert night. His voice had tightened. "Would you defend such a man, Durell?"

"I don't defend him. And I don't judge him. My orders are to take him back to Paris."

"You have no desire for revenge?"

"My personal feelings cannot enter into it," Durell said.

El-Abri looked at him curiously. "I ask you once more for this murderer, this assassin. I want this man who killed our mutual friend, who would have seen me killed along with my men, for personal gain. Two hours after he is in my hands, I promise to surrender. There will be an end to the fighting here. A small thing, perhaps, as I said before. I do not delude myself about my importance. But it is a straw, is it not?"

"You can surrender, anyway," Durell said. "Charles L'Heureux is of no importance in this matter."

"He is important to me. It is a matter of honor."

"I can't let you have him," Durell said.

The Kabyle turned away from the door of the *mechta*. His face had hardened. He looked as cruel as the barren land that had given him birth. "Durell, we are old friends. We fought together. You remember how it was, when we were young?"

Durell smiled. "I don't feel that old now."

"Still, it was many years ago. One grows old quickly in this land. And the world has changed. Your country can no longer walk in pride and solitary arrogance. You need friends. I do not like to speak to you in this fashion. Give me Charles L'Heureux."

"No."

"I cannot understand you."

Durell said, "I have my orders. Call it duty. I have to do my job."

"It is only that? A sense of duty?"

"Would you call that a small thing, Hadji?" Durell asked. "I don't enjoy having to protect this man. I didn't ask to save his life. But he must live to be tried justly and honestly, and then take his punishment. I'm taking him back to Paris with me."

"You were always·a stubborn man," the Hadji said softly. He looked at Durell with sadness behind his bold, tawny gaze. "It could be a stupidity. But I have one more thing to offer."

"The money?" Durell asked.

The Kabyle was surprised. He tried to hide it, but for just one moment the stony mask of his face gave way. He reached down on the floor and picked up a thermos bottle and poured two cups of coffee into small tin mugs. "What do you know about it?" el-Abri asked.

"I know that a quarter-of-a-million American dollars is floating around here somewhere. Do you have it, Hadji?"

"No."

"Do you know where it is?"

"I think so."

"Tell me about it," Durell said.

"The money was taken from your courier in a criminal plot," el-Abri said. "It had nothing to do with politics at the time. Then L'Heureux got into it through his associations with criminal gangs in this area and in the Mediterranean. Smugglers and the like. Scum and offal. The original thieves were killed. And the people for whom L'Heureux used to work got into it."

"Who are they?"

"Frenchmen," el-Abri said flatly. His voice rang harshly in the barren hut. "The types who, in their own way, are as bad as the rebel fanatics. The wealthy, the conservative territorials, landowners, businessmen

72

with vested interests in Algeria, who seek only to crush our reasonable aspirations with brutal force to keep us subservient. The day for that sort of thing is over, do you understand? There are elements in the extremists who might be called fascist, nationalist, racist, and there is a parallel element among the French."

"Where does the money come into it?"

"This certain French element wishes the money to be found publicly, under certain circumstances that would indicate your government is financing the extremists."

"That's ridiculous. Who would believe it?"

"Enough in France would believe it to whip up a frenzy of hate and violence. There would be a call to greater effort to crush the rebellion with force, terror, any brutal way at all. Conciliation, contact and negotiation would end. There would be no hope at all for a reasonable peace."

"It's a lot of money to throw away for that," Durell said.

"These people are rich. The money means nothing."

"It means something to L'Heureux. Has he planted it? Is that what you mean, Hadji? Is it ready to be discovered?"

"Yes."

"And you know where it is?"

"I can find it. For a price."

"For Charles L'Heureux?"

The Kabyle nodded. His eyes were bright and hard. "Yes."

"I can't let you have him," Durell said.

The guerrilla was silent for a moment. "We have been friends, Durell. You choose to be an enemy. Do you understand?"

"It is not my choice."

"I will have L'Heureux," el-Abri said. "You will not reach the coast with him. Not tonight or tomorrow. Not ever."

Durell stood up. The guard walked back and forth in front of the *mechta*. The night had suddenly grown colder. He went to the door and looked at the stars shining over the rocky desert. He looked at el-Abri. The Kabyle chieftain stood straight and tall, a dangerous man. His topaz eyes looked like stone in the cold light coming from the black sky.

73

"Will your driver take me back to the hotel now?" Durell asked.

"You came in peace. You may depart in peace. After that—" El-Abri shrugged. "I do not understand you at all, Durell. It is a small thing. A worthless life, against the saving of many lives."

"I have my job to do," Durell said.

"Then I shall have to kill you," the Kabyle said softly.

Chapter Eleven

JANE LARKIN was awake and dressed when Durell returned to the hotel. It was two o'clock in the morning. She heard the truck stop in the market place, and she looked down into the starlit darkness and saw Durell get out, followed by the slighter figure of Captain De-Grasse. A driver remained in the truck cab. The two men walked into the hotel entrance under her window.

Jane turned and looked toward the bed. "Chet?"

He lay on his back, hands clasped under his head. He stared at the ceiling and didn't reply.

"They're here, Chet. I'm sure he's going now, tonight."

"Good for him," Chet said.

"I'm going with him."

"No, Jane."

"With you or without you," she said.

He still didn't look at her, and that was the worst of it, she thought. "Please, Chet. We've quarreled all night. It's enough."

"We've quarreled all our life together."

"That's not my fault."

"Is it mine?"

"I don't know. I'm sorry."

She wondered what she was sorry about, really. Why should she feel like crying? It was over now, irrevocably finished. The dreams of girlhood, of one man forever, the scorn she once had of friends who married and divorced as if on a merry-go-round of thin and hysterical emotion. She had sworn it wouldn't be like that with Chet and herself. They would be different. Even old-fashioned. There was nothing wrong in being old-fashioned if it meant staying with one man for the rest of your life.

74

But it hadn't worked out like that. Everything was different. She hated this place, she was homesick; she hadn't reached that place in Chet where he lived and worked and laughed. She could have stayed in Algier. Algiers wasn't so bad. The French officers were charming, attentive. The shops on the Rue d'Isly were fun. But he had insisted that she meet him here in this god-forsaken village, halfway to the oil fields. The quarrel tonight had been the very worst, too. But nothing would change her mind. Even Algiers wasn't good enough now. She was going home, back to where things were safe and secure. With Chet or without him. If it had to be that way, then she couldn't help it. She wanted to hate him for his stubborn calm; but she wanted to weep.

She spoke to his silent figure. "I'm going to talk to Durell. I'm going to insist that he take me with him."

"All right," Chet said quietly.

"What do you mean, all right?"

"All right, I'll go with you."

"I thought you said your job—"

"You win," he said. "I'll quit. Are you satisfied?"

She wasn't. She didn't understand why she felt this stab of disappointment. She had won. She was going to have her way, after all. Chet would come back to Houston with her. But all at once she knew that this wasn't right, either. She didn't like this sudden, meek surrender. Daddy would have taken her over his knee and smacked some sense into her, according to his principles. But not Chet. Chet was always too gentle.

Damn, she thought, what's the matter with me?

She went into the corridor when she heard Durell's footsteps. He was with DeGrasse. Both men looked tense and angry, as if they had been arguing. Captain DeGrasse halted and his mouth smiled briefly.

"Mrs. Larkin. I thought you would be long asleep."

"I can't sleep. Neither can my husband. This raid tonight was the last straw." She was aware of Durell's eyes objectively appraising her. She heard the sound of her voice go on as if she accused DeGrasse of personal responsibility for the war here. "Please, captain. You told me yourself that Mr. Durell is going to try to reach the coast tonight."

"Not tonight," DeGrasse said.

"You have a truck out there. That's what it's for, isn't it? I insist you take my husband and me with you."

75

"Mrs. Larkin, you do not appreciate the dangers—"

"I can't stay here another minute. It's important. My daddy is worried enough already, and my husband's work here is finished, anyway. We've been waiting to go for days, and we won't be put off any longer."

"You have waited because I could not spare a detachment of men to safeguard your passage to Algiers. And I still cannot spare the men."

"But Mr. Durell is going."

"That is Durell's business. That is his job."

"I don't mind the danger. It can't be worse than right here."

DeGrasse looked helplessly at Durell. Durell hadn't spoken yet. He knew about the Larkins. Their presence in Marbruk had been worrying the Frenchman. On the way over in the truck, DeGrasse had tentatively asked if he would consider taking the Americans out of the danger zone, as a personal favor to him. Now Durell looked beyond Jane and saw Chet Larkin open his bedroom door and step into the hotel corridor. He appraised Chet quickly and accurately.

"I could use another gun," he said, "if Larkin understands the risks and is willing to accept them."

Chet Larkin nodded. "I know the dangers." He looked at Jane and then at DeGrasse. "The rebels will be busy in the hills tonight, licking their wounds. Now might be just the time to run for it. We could be in Algiers by noon."

DeGrasse looked harassed. "There is no open road. It will be most difficult. There may be an ambush waiting. How could I explain this to headquarters? It would be calamitous if anything went wrong."

"You needn't worry about us, captain," Chet said quietly. "We're willing to take our chances. My wife is very anxious to get back to the States in the shortest possible time." He looked at Durell. "You said you could use another gun. I'm a pretty good shot."

"You may have to be very good," Durell said.

"All right, then. I'm very good." Chet paused. "We're all packed and ready to go. I have no carbine, but I've a .38."

DeGrasse nodded reluctantly. "I can give you some automatic weapons. And you will need a driver. Talek, my man in the truck, knows all the routes to the coast. I can spare him."

Durell looked down the hallway. Madeleine Sardelle's door was only a few steps away. A new guard was on duty there. He turned back to DeGrasse. "Is Mlle. Sardelle safe?"

DeGrasse looked angry suddenly. "There are some things you could explain, you know. The first guard was knocked unconscious. You returned to the hotel a few moments afterward, and then Felix discovered you had gone out again and had locked the Sardelle girl in her room. Felix told me of all this. You were missing for almost two hours, m'sieu."

"Yes."

"Where did you go?"

"I visited an old friend," Durell said.

"Of the rebels, perhaps?"

"No."

"Then it was el-Abri."

"Perhaps."

DeGrasse looked coldly furious. "He has not surrendered yet, that type. I doubt if he will. It was all a trick. Or did he offer to negotiate again with you?"

"Not exactly," Durell said. "In any case, I gave my word not to speak of where I was or who I saw."

"I understand that my business is to fight the rebels," DeGrasse said bitterly. "I leave the politics to Paris, whatever mess they make of it. It is not for me to conduct mysterious expeditions to confer with old friends about old times. This belongs buried in the past."

"The roots of the past sometimes bear surprising fruit," Durell said. He looked at Jane Larkin. "You and your husband better get ready. I'll meet you both in the lobby in fifteen minutes."

Madeleine was awake. She sat on the edge of her bed, wearing slacks and a thin sweater against the dawning chill of the desert. She twisted to face Durell as he came in and closed the door.

"You're back, then," she said quietly. "Have you seen Charley?"

"I have him with me," Durell said. "We're going now."

Her body stiffened for an instant. She looked surprised, then displeased. "Now? Tonight? But the countryside will be too dangerous. Unless the plane has been repaired. . . ."

"We're going by truck." Durell's voice was flat. "Get ready now, please."

77

She demurred again. "But the rebels are aroused. I cannot see that Monsieur Brumont ordered us to risk the prisoner's safety by hurrying our departure this way. In a day or two, the situation will be clarified, the country-side around here will be pacified—"

"Were you counting on that?" Durell asked.

She met his gaze, then looked away. She drew a deep breath. "Durell, I want to explain why I was in your room earlier."

"You don't have to explain. I know why you were waiting for me, the way you were. It might have been interesting. It's regrettable that we had no chance to learn who could win on your field of battle."

She flushed. "No, you do not understand. I was lonely. I wanted—companionship. I was thinking of Charley. Where there is so much smoke, there must be fire, as you would say. Perhaps I've been blinded, because I care for him. But my job and my duty to Brumont—"

"Are you saying you have a change of heart?" he smiled.

"Is it not possible?"

"Not with you, honey," he said. "We've been operating under a truce, you and I. But I'm calling it off, as of now. Until we're in that truck, you don't leave my sight. You don't telephone or get in touch with Charley's friends."

"Very well." She stood up and picked up her small suitcase. Her red hair was coiled in two thick braids at the nape of her neck. Her slanted eyes regarded Durell with sudden wry amusement. "Our journey is not ended. Perhaps we can yet engage on my field of battle. Or are you faithful to your Miss Padgett?"

"Perhaps."

"You Americans are such fools when it comes to morality. What I was willing to offer was in loneliness, in search of simple friendship. With no strings attached. You do not believe what I say about Charley. You call us enemies now."

"Just so I know where I stand," Durell said shortly. "Let's go, shall we?"

Jane Larkin was aware of an odd excitement. She had walked outside to the hotel terrace with Chet, where the canvas-covered truck was parked facing the market place, and she had stood beside Chet in the chilly night air as their suitcases were placed in back of the vehicle.

The heavy tarpaulin over the troop carrier had been pulled open by the back flaps, and although she hadn't tried to peek, she had glanced inside.

She had been shocked to see Charles L'Heureux' pale, blazing eyes. She saw his face, his pale hair and scowling dark brows, and then she saw the quirk of his strong wide mouth as he laughed down at her and said softly, "Hi, baby. You're the Americans in town, huh?" His Maine accent was unmistakable. "Good to see a fellow-traveler, if you don't mind mixing the terms."

She didn't know what to say. His grin was sardonic as he held up handcuffed wrists. "I'm the prisoner you heard about, all right. No need to be afraid of me though, baby. Glad you're coming along. It might be a long, lonely ride."

"Where are they taking you?" Jane asked. She knew the question sounded inane. Somehow she hadn't thought about the prisoner as a tangible man. Certainly she hadn't expected him to be this big, arrogant man. "I mean, there have been all kinds of rumors about you. They say you shot another American here in town—"

Chet spoke angrily. "Jane, get away from there. Don't talk to him."

Something in his sharp tone made her suddenly contrary. She leaned forward over the truck tailgate to see the prisoner better in the interior dimness. He was sitting on one of two parallel benches running the length of the truck body under the canvas top.

L'Heureux grinned down at her. "Everything you heard about me is lies, baby. Do I look like a killer? I've been framed. It's only for political reasons, see? So who's the creep who gives you orders?"

"My husband," Jane said. She smiled. "We're riding to Algiers with you."

Chet pulled her away from the truck with an angry hand. "Jane, what's the matter with you?"

"I'm only talking to the man," she protested.

"You'll ride up front with Durell, understand?"

"Why can't I talk to him, Chet? What are you afraid of?"

"He should have been stood up against a wall and shot days ago. Just stay away from him, that's all," Chet said.

Jane moved away from the truck and sat down on the stone wall of the hotel terrace. The stars were beginning to fade in the segment of sky she could see over the Catholic convent across the market place. She heard L'Heureux' mocking laughter from the truck and remembered the glitter of his feral eyes. The bold and arrogant way the man had looked at her was strangely exciting. She shivered, but it was not from the chill desert wind that had sprung up recently. Then Chet returned to her.

"They say we're going to start off by heading south." He seemed troubled, and he carried a carbine DeGrasse had given him. He looked different, too, Jane thought. Chunky and somehow unreal with that rifle in his hand. As if it were all a game they were playing, unreal but exciting. Chet went on, "Durell thinks we ought to go in a wide circle and sweep back to the coast on the Farita road by daylight. He thinks we'll avoid any guerrilla ambushes that way, by starting out in the opposite direction."

"That sounds smart," Jane said.

Chet hesitated. "Jane, listen, I don't like any of it. We're safe here in Marbruk. This is crazy, rushing away before things settle down."

"Can you guarantee it will?"

"No, but—"

"Chet, I want to go home. I'm sick of this place. I'm up to here with it." Jane's voice sounded shrill, and she tried to soften her words. "I don't mind the danger. Besides, I'm sure nothing is going to happen to us. By tomorrow we'll be in Algiers and on the plane to France and then home."

Chet looked at her with an expression she did not understand. His jaw looked square and hard and angry. "Does home in Texas mean that much to you, Jane?"

"Of course."

Durell was coming down the steps from the hotel. Madeleine was with him. "If you're all ready," he said, "we can get started."

Chapter Twelve

CHET requested that Jane sit up front in the cab with Durell and the *goumier*, Talek. The Arab driver was a small, slight man with a narrow face and a bad scar over one eye, but he looked smart and military in the uniform of the special native troops used by the French Army. Durell watched Madeleine greet Charley as she climbed in the back with Chet. Their words were brief and cool, a meaningless exchange of formalities. He wished he could see the girl's face more clearly, but the interior of the truck was too gloomy. He ordered Madeleine to sit across from L'Heureux, and told Chet privately to keep them that way. Chet sat near the tailgate, where he could watch the road unwinding behind the truck.

The air blowing through the open cab windows was cold, but the light was strengthening in the east. With the rising sun, the weight of the Sahara heat would return in full violence.

Talek's carbine was in a rack in the cab ceiling, overhead. Durell kept his rifle in his lap. Jane peered through the windshield, but she could see nothing alarming in the landscape. Her few attempts to question Durell about the prisoner in the truck were met with quiet evasions.

"Aren't we wasting precious time and mileage this way?" she demanded.

"It may be the best way to avoid the rebels."

"But even if we went directly, it would take four hours to reach the coast," she objected. "Going this way, we won't make it until late afternoon. This pokey old truck doesn't go much over thirty."

"Sometimes the straightest distance between two points can be the long way around," Durell said.

"I'm sorry. I shouldn't interfere. It's just that I'm so anxious to get home," Jane said.

She turned her head and looked through the flap into the interior of the truck. The first thing she saw was Charles L'Heureux' eyes. He grinned at her. All she could see of Chet was his shoulder and the back of his head as he leaned forward on the bench to keep a lookout through the rear flap. The French girl, Madeleine, sat stiffly across from the prisoner. There was something in the way Madeleine looked and smiled quietly at L'Heureux that made Jane wonder if they knew each other better than they pretended. A surprising touch of envy moved in her and shocked her.

Chet had been the only man in her life, and it was natural, she thought, to wonder what other men might

81

be like. How could she judge, if she had no other stand-ards by which to judge the man she had married? Jane turned back and faced front, clenching her hands.

She shouldn't be thinking like this, she told herself. It was wrong, no matter how far apart she and Chet had drifted. It was this strange country, she decided, the heat and the fighting and the hatreds that made the very air electric with odd tensions.

The light grew stronger in the east. The rocky scarps and defiles opening on either side of the road grew sharper in outline. Durell spread a military map on his knees over the carbine he held and studied it. He spoke to Talek, the Arab driver.

"We should be about ten kilometers from the village of Baroumi," he said.

"Yes, sir."

"There's a trace here off to the west that seems to cut through to the coastbound road. Can we use it?"

"It is very rough, sir. Very wild country."

"Any guerrillas in it?"

"No rebels have been reported, sir."

"Suppose we take it and hole up for a rest, just before we reach the *douar*. It should be scouted before we go through any village."

"Yes, sir. But we ought to cover as much ground as we can while it's still cool."

"We'll do that," Durell agreed.

The light grew stronger. Talek turned the truck into a narrow wadi that had a fairly flat floor to it and faint tracks made by other vehicles in the past. The rising sun was behind them now. Jane felt suddenly sleepy. The jolting of the truck and the steady thrum of the engine made the restless night just past seem a night-mare in retrospect. She wanted to look back into the truck body again, but somehow she was afraid that if she did, the first thing she would meet would be the prisoner's knowing eyes. She leaned her head back and tried to sleep.

When she awoke, the truck had stopped. She was alone in the cab of the truck, and seeing this, panic touched her. There was no one around. It was broad daylight now, almost nine o'clock, and the sun's heat struck viciously at her, glancing off the walls of the rocky cul-de-sac where they had halted. Red and yel-low sandstone cliffs, barren of even the slightest trace of green, towered on three sides. She felt hot and sticky with perspiration.

"Chet?" she called quickly.

"Here, honey."

She turned and saw him walking across the rocky floor of the ravine. He carried his carbine easily, as if he were familiar with it, and somehow he looked different. Perversely, she was annoyed at the prompt way he popped up, as if he had been hovering solicitously over her. Jane got down out of the cab and shook out her tangled blond hair and lifted her arms over her head to stretch. She saw Charley L'Heureux watching her. His eyes were boldly appraising her breasts. She dropped her arms and turned away with a flush of angry embarrassment, but not before she caught his quick, knowing grin.

"Why have we stopped, Chet?"

"It's just for a rest. I've been detailed to scout ahead. The main road to Baroumi is just ahead, and Durell wants me to walk along it for a way to see if there are any signs of the rebels in the neighborhood."

She looked at him. "You enjoy this, don't you? Playing soldier again, I mean."

"Jane, this is dangerous territory."

"Who'd be hanging around this desolate place? It's crazy. We ought to keep right on going."

"Durell knows what he's doing," Chet said. "Are you all right, honey?"

"Of course I'm all right. I'm fine. I'm hot and sticky and hungry and thirsty and I've had no sleep for ages. I'm just dandy."

"I'll be back in half an hour," he said.

"Don't get sunstroke," she called caustically.

He turned away. Durell and Talek were standing on one of the low cliff edges above her and to the east. Durell was looking at something through field glasses, and Talek stood beside him with a tommy gun in his hands. Nothing stirred except the shimmering heat waves that glanced off the glitter of sand and rock. Now that she had mentioned it, she did feel very thirsty. There were some canteens of water in the back end of the truck, and she walked around to it and drank heavily.

Charley L'Heureux stood beside her. His hands looked strange in the cuffs that bound him. "Take it easy, baby. Just wet your lips. That's the way to do it out here."

"There's plenty of water," she said.

"Plenty for today."

"By tonight we'll all be in Algiers," Jane said.

"I don't think so."

She stared at him. "No?"

"Do you trust this Durell?" he asked quietly.

"I don't know," she said. She felt a stir of alarm. She wished he wouldn't look at her so arrogantly. "Why shouldn't I?"

"He thinks he's smart, cutting south like this. We're in the heart of rebel country."

"Are you trying to frighten me?"

"Just telling you, is all."

"Those people won't bother us. I'm American."

"You're from Texas, huh? I can always tell a Texas woman."

"I'm from Houston," she said.

"That's a wonderful town," L'Heureux said. "I spent a lot of time there. Long ago, before they shipped us out in the war. I always wanted to go back. Lots of action in Houston. Good food, good hotels, plenty of wonderful women. But none of them as pretty as you, Jane."

She looked at his handcuffed wrists. "What did you do? Did you really kill that man named Boston?"

"It was in self-defense," he said easily.

"You don't seem worried about going back for a trial."

"There won't be any trial," L'Heureux said quietly. His teeth were white and even when he smiled. She was struck again by the strange contrast between his sun-bleached hair that was almost white, cropped short like a college boy's, and his thick shaggy black brows. There was a smell clinging to his khaki shirt and trousers—the smell of prison, and more. The smell of sweat and manliness. Chet had never smelled like that. She shivered. "You *are* trying to frighten me, aren't you?"

"Nothing's going to happen to you, Jane," he said. "I'll see to that. What do you say we take a walk and stretch our legs?"

Jane looked up the sandstone cliff to where Durell and Talek made dark, distant silhouettes against the brazen sky. "Will he let you wander around loose?"

L'Heureux held up his handcuffed wrists. "I can't go far like this, can I? And I wouldn't want to. Not in this country. He knows I've got to stick close to the truck."

Jane looked across the little clearing to where Madeleine, the French girl, was combing her hair and staring bluntly at them. The redheaded girl looked sullen and angry. "What about her? I understand she's your girl. Why is she here?"

"She came along for the ride. Come on, walk with me."

"Won't she be jealous?"

He grinned. "Now why should you say that?" His eyes were brazen with feigned innocence. "What would she have to be jealous about? My hands are tied, ain't they?"

She met his eyes. She flushed. He was laughing at her because she had given something away without meaning to, and he knew it and was way ahead of her. "Come on," he said again. "A little walk up the wadi won't break any eggs."

She began to walk with him without thinking about it. "Now you've reminded me," she said lightly, "I'm so darned hungry. Doesn't this caravan serve any breakfast?"

"Cold chicken. Cold coffee. Coming up in twenty minutes, when your husband comes back. He's been appointed cook, I reckon." L'Heureux laughed softly. "Incidentally, what's he always so sore about? Like he got a bee in his pants. You quarreled with him, or something?"

"A little," she admitted.

"Poor jerk. And I was beginning to envy him. Having you and Texas and all that, while I'm being carted away to face a firing squad or the guillotine or electric chair, if they get me that far."

"You don't seem such a terribly dangerous man to me."

"You're lying, Jane. You're afraid of me."

She bit her lip. "I can't seem to keep any secrets from you, can I?"

"Before this trip is over, you won't have any left at all, I promise you."

"Are you sure that's a promise? It sounds threatening."

He grinned lightly. "Make what you want of it, honey."

They came to a bend in the wadi and walked around a wall of sandstone, and the truck was cut off from sight behind them. Jane wanted to look back to see if Madeleine was following, or if Chet had returned, but she didn't. L'Heureux was holding his handcuffed wrists out before him.

"I wish I wasn't handicapped like this, Jane. It's been a long time since I went strolling with a girl like you."

"You assume too much," Jane said.

"Do I? I know you. I know your kind. Let's sit down in the shade a minute. Tell me all about Texas and your daddy's oil wells. He's got oil wells, hasn't he?"

"Yes."

"So you're very rich."

"Yes," she said simply.

"And you're bored with that creep of a husband, huh?"

She said quickly, "Chet isn't like that." She paused as L'Heureux grinned at her. "All right, yes, I'm bored."

"Maybe you've been seeing the country with the wrong party. Africa is pretty exciting. And profitable. I'm an old hand at it, you know. I could show you things that would make you forget ever to be bored again."

"I suppose you could," she murmured.

"But not with my hands tied."

She looked at him. "You're very obvious, Charley. If you think you can talk me into helping you get loose, you're presumptuous, conceited, and stupid."

"Oh, I'm conceited all right." His laughter made thick bubbles in his throat. "But not stupid, baby. What do you think would happen if I got my hands loose, huh?"

"It won't happen. Not with my help."

"You're afraid to think about that, right?"

"I think we'd better go back now," Jane said.

"Look at me," he said sharply.

She looked away. She couldn't see the truck. She thought she saw someone moving on the lip of rock overhanging the wadi back there, but she couldn't be sure. It was probably Durell, keeping an eye on his prisoner.

"Look," L'Heureux said, standing behind her.

Then she felt his hands on her body.

The shock of knowing that his hands, incredibly, were free was paralyzing. His fingers dug brutally into the soft flesh of her waist. She wanted to cry out. His grip was too painful to stand. But she didn't cry out. She sucked in her breath and was silent. She felt herself turned forcibly around to face him. She felt herself pulled hard against his massive, sweaty body.

"Don't scream, Jane," he whispered.

"How did you—how did you do it?" she gasped.

"I've been free for half an hour. Pretty good, huh? I just kept the shackles on to make it look good."

"Let me go! You're hurting me. I *will* scream."

"You asked for it, didn't you? You walked out here with me, didn't you? Looking for kicks, huh?" He laughed

silently down at her as she tried to twist free of his powerful hands. "Go ahead and yell. Yell for your husband. Yell
for Durell. Why don't you?"

"What do you want?" she whispered fiercely.

"I'm walking away from here, baby. Don't you want to
take a walk with me? It's a whole new world for you out
there. I'll have money, plenty of it. You don't have to
worry about that. Look, I know your kind, I know what
you want, and I can give it to you. Lots of excitement,
lots of thrills, and no strings attached. I'll see to that,
Jane."

She said slowly, "You must be insane. How did you get
those handcuffs off?"

He shook the steel rings free of his wrist. They made
flat clinking sounds on the rocky ledge where they stood.
"What difference does it make?"

All at once he bent his head and kissed her. His stubbly
dark beard scraped her face. His mouth was hard an
painful on her lips. She felt suffocated by his huge male-
ness. Her heart hammered crazily. She pummeled at hi.
chest with her fists. She was afraid. She had gone too far.
Why had she walked out here with this man, this murderer? She felt herself thrown roughly to the hard ground.
She wasn't sure what was happening. The brazen sky
reeled over her head.

She screamed as he searched her body.

There was a sound of running footsteps. A small slide
of falling gravel struck her legs as someone came down
the shale slope from the top of the ledge. L'Heureux released her. She pulled her body together from somewhere
far out, where it had started to go, and stood up. She felt
weak and sick. She saw the prisoner's body as something
huge and black and defiant, standing against the blinding
glare of the sun.

"Don't move, Charley."

It was Durell. Jane turned her head as if her neck hurt
her. It did. Durell had a gun in his hand. Jane's legs
trembled. She still felt L'Heureux' weight upon her. She
pushed her hair back from her face. Durell wasn't even
looking at her when he spoke to L'Heureux.

"Did she let you go?"

"Ask her," L'Heureux said. He grinned his wolfish grin.

"I didn't," Jane whispered. "How could I? Believe me."

"Are you hurt?" Durell asked. He still didn't look at her.

"No. No, I guess not. It was so quick—"

"You've been very foolish. Go back to the truck, please."

"I'll see you later, Jane," L'Heureux said casually. He looked at Durell. "Go ahead, use the gun. I'm walking out of here, pal."

"Try it."

"You ain't going to shoot me," L'Heureux said. "You've got to take me back to your pals alive, right? You won't use the gun."

"I'll bring you back. But not all in one piece. A broken kneecap won't keep you from talking when we get to Paris. But it will keep you from running off. Don't tempt me, Charley."

Jane watched, fascinated. The two men stood several feet apart. Durell's face was dark and angry, and she thought his anger went beyond what had happened to her. It was as if he were disappointed about something. Something he had wanted to happen, and which hadn't happened. L'Heureux lost some of his bold confidence as he met Durell's eyes. He licked his lips.

"Hell, I guess you'd gimp me, at that."

"Just don't ask for it," Durell said. "Go on back to the truck."

Charley grinned. "Hell, I guess I will. I ain't had breakfast yet, anyway."

Chet came running down the narrow wadi toward them. His khaki shirt was streaked with sweat from his walk in the desert sun. There were deep lines of alarm and rage in his youthful face.

"Are you all right, Jane?"

"Yes," she whispered.

"What happened? What did he try to do to you?"

L'Heureux said, "What do you think, boy?"

A muscle jumped in Chet's throat. He made an inarticulate sound of anger and then he jumped at the prisoner with no further warning. Durell's sharp command came too late. Chet's fist made a flat sound as it struck the prisoner's jaw. L'Heureux did not move. His body was like a rock. He laughed and his left hand shot out and stiff fingers jabbed at Chet's throat with amazing speed. Chet fell backward, twisting, and then doubled forward as he clawed at his neck. L'Heureux stepped toward him and his right fist slammed at Chet; Chet went down as if under a cleaver. He rolled over and over on the rocky floor of the ravine. Durell moved in.

"That's enough, Charley."

"He asked for it, the boy scout."

"He doesn't know how to fight your way. Leave him alone. He's her husband."

Jane felt paralyzed. She looked at Chet, on the ground, humiliated and beaten so suddenly that it was difficult to think of what had happened. L'Heureux wasn't even breathing hard. She watched Durell pick up Chet's carbine and throw it aside where L'Heureux couldn't reach it. Durell still looked disappointed, as if what was happening was not what he had really wanted to happen. Jane went to Chet and knelt beside him.

"Chet?" Her voice was small and thin. "Chet, get up."

"Get away from me," he whispered.

"Chet, I'm sorry—"

He jerked away and stood wavering on his feet. She put her arm around him to help. He pulled away, not looking at her. She couldn't see his face. He kept rubbing his throat. Without looking at Durell or L'Heureux, Chet walked away on uncertain feet, down the wadi to where they had left the truck.

Durell turned to Jane. "Go on, go with him."

"He doesn't want me," she said helplessly.

"He will. Stay with him. He's been hurt in more ways than one."

L'Heureux laughed. "The punk ought to learn to be a man, if he wants to keep his woman in this country."

"Shut up," Durell said. "Let's go."

The truck was still parked in the shade under the cliff where they had left it. Madeleine was on her feet beside the tailgate, shading her eyes against the sun as she watched them return. A hot wind funneled down the wadi and fluttered the short sleeves of her blouse. Her mouth thinned as she saw L'Heureux walking back a few steps ahead of Durell. She looked at Jane and Chet, and anger tightened the fine planes of her face. "Charley?"

"It's all right, Mad. It just didn't come off."

"What happened? I gave you your chance."

He patted her cheek. "I got distracted, is all."

"By that girl?"

"Sure, by the girl." He shrugged. "Don't go making noises at me, Mad." His French was laced with a strong Canuck accent.

"You threw away your chance to escape because of this girl?" Madeleine's voice trembled with anger. She looked venomous. She yanked her arm free when L'Heureux held

89

it. "You fool! I did what I could for you! It was going to be so simple—"

"Too simple, Mad. Where did you get the key to those bracelets?"

She looked defiantly at Durell. "I took them from him."

"You think you got light fingers, eh?" L'Heureux turned to Durell. "You knew she swiped the key from you, didn't you? She thinks she's good. She's had lots of training picking pockets. She worked that racket for a long time in Algiers and Marseilles, before she got to Paris and took the modeling job and then worked for Brumont. Is she really good, Durell?"

Durell said flatly, "Good enough."

"You knew she took the key off you, didn't you? You let her have it. I know you, Durell. Nobody could lift anything off you unless you wanted it to happen. It was too easy. Why did you want me to get away?"

"You can figure that out for yourself," Durell said.

"Not to kill me while I was escaping. You don't want that."

"No."

L'Heureux started to speak again, then shut his mouth into a hard, angry line. He muttered, "I guess maybe I got to figure you a little differently, Durell."

He climbed into the truck and stretched out on one of the benches. Madeleine stared at Durell in defiance. "You yourself ended our truce. I told you how I feel about Charley. I warned you I would help him." She drew a deep, uncertain breath. The sun made burnished gold in her red hair. "Did you know when I stole the key from you? Is Charley right?"

"Yes," Durell said. "But you'll sit up front with me from now on, Madeleine." He reached into the truck and found a coil of rope and handed it to Chet Larkin. "Tie him up. Wrists behind his back this time. Make the knots strong. Can you do it?"

"My pleasure," Chet muttered.

"Don't feel ashamed because he put you down," Durell said. "He's put down better men than you."

Chet said nothing. L'Heureux sat up on the truck bench and was impassive as Chet bound his wrists with the rope. The sun had reached up high in the sky now and they stood in the full glare of its terrible heat as Durell waited for Chet to jump down from the tailgate.

"Was the road ahead clear?" Durell asked.

"I didn't see anything. There's nothing alive out that way."

"All right. We'll eat while we're riding. You and your wife stay in the back here with L'Heureux. Keep him on one side, you stay on the other. Here's your carbine. Keep it trained on him."

Durell walked around to the front of the truck and searched the wadi for Talek, the *goumier* driver. He had left the Arab on watch at the top of the cliff. There was no sign of the man.

"Talek!"

His voice echoed down the rocky ravine and was lost in the wilderness of sun and stone. There was no answer. He searched the ravine with his eyes. The hot wind came in quickening gusts, and sand hissed along the stones at his feet.

"Talek!"

Madeleine got out of the truck and stared ahead, her face showing nothing. Durell walked away up the wadi, to where it opened onto a flat area of terrain bisected by the thin, fragile line of a highway arrowing north and south. Telephone poles and lines stood forlornly in the blazing sun. Durell knew the lines had been cut, although they looked all right in this particular spot. The main road that Chet had scouted was of crushed stone, raised a little on a two-foot embankment above the level of the desert floor. There was nothing in sight in either direction. No sign of the *goumier* driver. He turned and walked back to the truck.

Madeleine still stood by the cab, not looking at him.

"He's gone," she said flatly.

"How do you know?"

"He looked at the motor and walked off, while you were with Charley back there."

"Which way did he go?"

She pointed toward the bleak highway ahead. "There."

Durell went around to the front of the truck and lifted the hood. Even before he examined the engine, he knew what he would find.

The distributor cap was gone.

There was no way to start the truck. They were stranded.

Chapter Thirteen

DURELL took a cup of coffee from the thermos Jane Larkin handed him. There was a knapsack of sandwiches and two bottles of Algerian wine and a bottle of Martel. There was a gallon thermos jug of water that Talek had failed to pour out onto the sand, and Durell thought grimly that he should be grateful for small favors. The rest of the picture was clear enough. Talek had betrayed them. He belonged to the rebels and had enlisted with the French only to act as a spy for the guerrillas. But the big question was whether he worked for the extremists or for el-Abri's forces. The answer here was important. It might mean the difference between life and death.

Durell sipped his coffee slowly. In this business you took calculated risks time and again, judging the chances on the weight of all the facts you could gather in hand. Now and then, however, all your best calculations could be upset by something totally unlooked for. Such as Jane Larkin. He hadn't expected her to interfere with Charley the way she had. If she hadn't screamed, Durell would not have interrupted the scene.

He had deliberately made it easy for Madeleine to steal the handcuff keys. Perhaps too easy. L'Heureux had caught on to that maneuver. But it was doubtful if he had suspected it until the very last moment.

Not that Durell wanted L'Heureux to escape. But his job here went beyond simply escorting the man back to civilization and adequate punishment. There was all that American currency floating around the area. The money wasn't important in itself. The thing that was important was what the money might do. He hadn't forgotten a single word el-Abri had told him about the money. He had been thinking about it ever since.

There were Frenchmen in Algiers who profited by this war, who might wish to prolong it or to win it without compromise, without yielding to any single one legitimate aspiration of the other side. It was to their advantage to fan the fires of terror and violence to the point where no compromise could be effected.

Finding the American money in the hands of the rebels

could do that. Propaganda could make much of it, all wrong. The United States could be accused of secretly financing and abetting the rebellion, perhaps on a deal to gain certain oil concessions in the Sahara. It was not too fantastic that some of the inflamed and angry and tormented men would believe it. If pressure were being exerted by the saner, more rational men in this country to end the war, such a propaganda campaign could make them close ranks, join the shadowy few without understanding how they were being manipulated, and the war would go on and on, without visible end.

The money had to be found, and quickly.

It had to be removed quietly, returned to the proper authorities.

Durell had narrowed his thinking down to one point. L'Heureux knew where the money was hidden. There wasn't time to take him back to Paris and interrogate him and hope to get that information from him. L'Heureux had his own goal. He wanted the money for himself. He was playing a dangerous double game, one he would inevitably lose, because if he crossed the men who had hired him and stole the money, they would certainly track him down. There would be no corner of the world too remote for him to remain in hiding from those who would search for him. But L'Heureux didn't know that. Or if he knew it, he was still confident.

The nub of the thing was the lack of time. L'Heureux had to be made to lead him to the money, and quickly. He had hoped that by letting Madeleine free him, L'Heureux would take off and make for the place where it would be found. A calculated risk, and one that had gone wrong.

Now there was the stranding here with a useless truck.

Durell sipped again at his coffee, thinking it out. It had been twenty minutes since Talek disappeared. It was possible to pursue him, and an even chance they could overtake him and retrieve the distributor cap. But Durell knew his own limitations in this wasteland. First, there was no way to guess which direction Talek had chosen. You couldn't track a man for any distance in this rocky terrain. And obviously, Talek's chances for survival were better than their own. He knew where he was going. He knew where he could meet the rebels. He had only taken one canteen of water, so his destination couldn't be too far off.

According to the chart Captain DeGrasse had given him, the nearest place was the oasis village of Baroumi, ten miles southwest of here. Ten miles was not far for truck travel. But it might be impossible to get there on foot. There was L'Heureux and the need for watchfulness, and there were the two women. He didn't know if he could push them along on a ten-mile walk in this heat and desolation. He knew he could count on Chet Larkin. He didn't underestimate Chet simply because L'Heureux had beaten him so quickly and viciously. Chet would be careful now. He could be of help. Still, ten miles wasn't easy. They'd need luck if they could make it.

And even if they reached Baroumi, Durell thought, there was no guessing at their reception. The Moslems there could be rebels, or they could be loyal. Or they might owe their allegiance to el-Abri, which was even more likely. Certainly they would be armed and suspicious.

But there was also the reasonable certainty that somewhere in the village there would be a vehicle of one kind or another.

There was no other place to go.

It had to be Baroumi.

Durell uncorked the brandy bottle and added a small slug of liquor to the coffee remaining in his cup, and finished the sandwich Jane Larkin had given him. The others were huddled in the thin slab of shade cast by the truck body. They looked reluctant to leave even the brief familiarity and illusion of safety the truck gave them. L'Heureux alone seemed comfortable and unconcerned. He sat with his back against a rear wheel and had his eyes closed. Madeleine stood a little distance from him. Jane Larkin was trying to talk to her husband, but Chet had his back turned to her. The boy had been badly hurt by his wife's behavior, Durell thought. But he would get over that. They would all have to pull together and cooperate if they had any hope of getting away from here alive.

He looked at Jane's shoes. They were oxfords, of dark brown leather, and sensible enough. Her lightweight slacks and blouse would give her reasonable protection against the sun. Chet wore boots. L'Heureux had been given Army-issue shoes, tough and sturdy. Madeleine wore low-heeled shoes, too. They were all right in that respect, at any rate.

Jane looked up and walked over to him.

"What are we going to do? We can't stay here, can we?"

"We're going to have to walk out of it. Can you make it?"

"Back to Marbruk?"

"That's twenty miles," he said. "I doubt if we'd last. No, we can go on to Baroumi. It's a little village not too far ahead. I was there once, as a matter of fact, during the war." Durell paused. "If we're lucky, we might find a car or jeep we could use."

"But the guerrillas might be there, too," she objected. There was still a trace of shock and confusion in her eyes, but her voice was steady, almost defiant. "What do we do then?"

"We'll hide out and try to steal something without getting caught." He smiled at her and saw her mouth lift in response. It was only a small sign, but it gave him more confidence in her. "Do you think you can walk ten kilometers?"

"Yes, I can do it," she said.

"Better stay with your husband while we're hiking," Durell said. "He can cover you if something breaks wrong."

"He doesn't want me near him. Nothing happened, you know, but he thinks it was my fault."

"He'll get over it. You'll have to help each other. I'm counting on Chet to keep an eye on L'Heureux from here on out. Each of you will have to carry something, too. Water, the thermos jugs, the knapsack." Durell turned. "Madeleine?"

"I am here," the redheaded girl said. "I understand what is needed."

He met her topaz eyes. Hostility had died in them. She knew what they faced. The distance didn't seem too much, perhaps a three- or four-hour hike. But across this wasteland, the road could seem infinite.

"Did you know about Talek?" he asked.

"No. Not that."

"How soon do you think the rebels will come back for us?" He was curious to know what her thoughts might be.

"Perhaps they will not come here at all," Madeleine said. "They may leave it to the sun and the desert to do their work for them."

"Maybe. What do you know about Baroumi?"

"I have never been there."

"Let's hope you get a look at it today."

She looked down at her feet and drew a deep breath. She seemed to be having trouble meeting Durell's eyes. "I know something about the place, though." The hot, scorching wind blew her red hair. Her face looked pale, shining with perspiration. Her Paris glamor had worn off, along with the brittle sophistication she had exhibited when they first met. Something much more elemental lurked under her smooth, tawny flesh as she walked around the truck with him. "Charley has been to Baroumi," she said suddenly.

"How do you know?"

"He spoke it earlier. It is where he would like to go. That is why you let me steal the handcuff keys from you, is it not? So you could track him while he imagined he was escaping. Well, that isn't necessary now. You see, I am being honest with you. He wants to go to Baroumi."

"Why?" Durell asked. "What's there for him?"

"It is the money," she said flatly. Her voice was lacking in spirit all at once. "You know about it. Why play games with me? You are more clever than I can ever hope to be. And better than Charley in this business. I can see that now."

Durell studied the girl's face, then looked at Jane. Jane was watching L'Heureux, still sprawled in the shade cast by the disabled truck.

Madeleine's voice shook slightly. "Charley tried to take Jane with him, didn't he? He has me, but I am not enough. He is so sure of me, so confident that I will help him and do anything and ask no questions. He thinks I will always accept the crumbs he cares to throw my way. He thinks he knows me, you see. But he is mistaken. He doesn't know me at all. You and I, Durell, are much more alike. We understand each other, you and I. And you have no illusions about me, which is a better basis for understanding than Charley's attitude toward women."

"You knew what L'Heureux was like when you sold out to him," Durell said. "You crossed Brumont and the Deuxième Bureau when they assigned you to work on him. You said you were in love with L'Heureux."

"I know nothing about love," she said curtly. "You

96

Americans are much too romantic. I know all about men, but I know nothing of love. It does not exist. Passion, yes. I know what it is to want someone. But this is not love. And Charley has never loved me."

"You tried to help him escape."

"I was willing to help him up to that point, yes. Because it was really for myself that I did these things. But he threw away his chance because of a pretty face and a new figure. He doesn't fool me by saying he was suspicious of your intentions. It was that Jane. His conceit is limitless. He thinks I will accept his foolish mistake and forget about it and humbly creep back to him when he crooks his little finger for me. But he is mistaken."

"Tell me about the money," Durell said. "Do you think it's in Baroumi?"

"I am sure of it."

"Where can it be found?"

Her eyes were pale gold, narrowed against the hot sunshine. "First tell me why you are here in Algeria. What happens here should be of no concern to Americans. There is an honest movement here toward freedom. We want to be equal with others in the world. Who are you to condemn it and work against it?"

"We don't condemn. We don't act for or against it," Durell said. "I'm here to take a murderer back to justice. The fact that he happens to have been your lover is not my business. Your own foolishness tied your fate to his, Madeleine. If he happens to have the morals and lusts of an alley cat, that too is your problem, not mine."

"I want to help you," she said suddenly.

"Because you're angry with Charley now? You'll get over that, I think," Durell said.

She shook her head. "No, you do not understand. I know the truth now. I know it was only a dream, an illusion, this plan I had with Charley. We were going to take the money and go to South America with it. It is what I have always dreamed of. But now I know what would really happen if we were successful. He would leave me. Perhaps he would kill me. The first pretty woman to come along would make him throw me aside." Madeleine's voice caught. "I was a fool to think I could control a man like Charley. Some men are easy, but others, I have learned, are best avoided. Perhaps I wanted to believe that it would be all right with Charley. But I know better now. I saw how he looked at Jane. I know he has no

97

more use for me. I am an expert on how men think, Durell. I am not wrong."

"So now you turn against him."

She shrugged. "What would you have me do? I hope to salvage what I can. Perhaps you will help me when you see Brumont again."

"How long will your feeling last?" he asked. "How long can I trust you?"

"You will have to take your chances with that. I am not lying to you now. You want to know where the money is?"

"Do you know?"

"Of course. It is in a well somewhere in the vicinity of the house of the parents of Hadji el-Abri."

Durell stared at her. "They live in Baroumi. I know that. But I don't believe el-Abri is in on the scheme of those who want to use the money to prolong the war here."

"He is not. He knows nothing about it. He may suspect the money is in Baroumi, but Charley fooled him by putting the money so close to his own home. You'll find the money there. You can be sure of that."

Durell looked up at Jane and Chet Larkin. Chet had strapped the knapsack of food to his back, and Jane was carrying the water thermos. They were ready to move out.

He ordered L'Heureux to walk about ten paces ahead. The prisoner objected that it was too difficult for him to walk with his hands tied behind his back, but Durell did not change the arrangement.

They followed the main road bearing away to the right. It was ten o'clock when they set out, and the sun was already intolerable. Durell ordered them all off the road for a distance of about a hundred yards and they walked parallel to it. Sometimes it was in sight, but most often not. Nothing stirred or seemed to live in the rocky wilderness.

There was no talking among them. Just the effort to keep breathing and walking took all their concentration. The air was like the exhaust from a blast furnace. The heat scorched their mouths and lips and throats and left their lungs gasping for coolness. Thirst came quickly. Durell kept his eyes on L'Heureux. The prisoner's massive figure moved with a long, awkward stride, his hands behind his back. L'Heureux seemed to be totally unaware of the heat and the wasteland they crossed.

The terrain dipped and rose, dipped and rose again. They were climbing gradually. Here and there were patches of blinding sand, like shimmering pools caught in the arms of wind-hewn rock. The highway was empty every time Durell glimpsed it. It reached from horizon to horizon, the long line of telephone poles marching parallel to it, going nowhere, coming from nowhere.

It came to him that this was the way the end of the world might look. A scorched, lifeless, rocky emptiness, with only a few straggling, hopeless survivors wandering aimlessly in search of something that would never be again. He shook off the image.

They walked on. Once he paused when he saw the copper lines dangling uselessly from the insulators on the power poles. They saw two more places where communications had been cut by the rebels. In some stretches, the wire itself had been totally removed.

After half an hour, Durell called a ten-minute halt. L'Heureux leaned easily against the rocky face of a small cliff that offered some dubious shade. His heavy face was sardonic, his pale eyes fixed on Durell.

"They won't ever make it, chum. Just look at 'em."

Durell saw that Jane Larkin was already in unpromising shape. Her hair was disheveled and her face looked sunken, shining and pale. Her mouth was open as she breathed tumultuously. She sank down to the ground as if she never intended to get up again.

Madeleine was only a little better. Chet sat leaning forward, the carbine between his knees, the muzzle pointed at the brassy sky. His eyes were fixed on his wife with a curious mixture of hunger and rejection.

"They'll make it," Durell said.

"We've only covered about two kilometers."

"We have all day."

"We walk into Baroumi like this, and we're just meat for the buzzards, you know that?"

"We'll see."

Durell passed the thermos of water around. He kept the container of water, slinging it over his shoulder by the canvas straps. It already weighed too much for Jane Larkin to continue to carry it.

When the ten minutes were up, he ordered them to their feet. They stood in a straggling, silent, and reluctant group. He knew that at the next stop it would be more difficult to get them going again, and the one after that might prove impossible.

He walked beside the prisoner for a short time.

"Durell, you're a fool," L'Heureux said. "You should have stayed with the truck."

"And let Talek bring your murdering friends down on us?"

"I don't know anything about that gook."

"On the other hand," Durell said, "he might be one of el-Abri's men. In that case, you ought to be glad to get away from that spot."

"I've got nothing to worry about," L'Heureux said. His glance was bold. "I told you, I'm an innocent man. You're the lad who's in a tough spot. You took on the responsibility of them two babes in the wood from the States. They're both helpless and hopeless. They'll only hold you back. And Madeleine is on my side. I know she's sore at me, but don't count on that to help you. She'll do what I tell her, when I get around to it."

"I doubt that."

L'Heureux laughed softly. "You hate my guts, huh?"

"Yes, I do."

"But you've got to take care of me, Durell. You've got to make sure I get back home alive, huh?"

"I'll get you there."

"But all the odds are on my side." The prisoner moved his head in a gesture that encompassed the bleak, sun-blasted landscape. "You can't kill me, but I've got nothing holding me back when it comes to taking care of you."

"Do you still think you've got a chance to get away with that money?" Durell asked suddenly.

L'Heureux broke his long, rhythmic stride momentarily. He laughed. "Did Madeleine tell you about that?"

"I knew about it from other sources, as well."

"Did she tell you where it is?"

"Yes. How did you get into that game?"

The prisoner shrugged. "It's my business. I'm for hire."

"Who hired you?"

"Some pretty big people."

"In Paris?"

"And Algiers."

"They want to make it look as if the United States, or American oil interests, is financing the rebels.

"Sure. That's all they need to make the average
100

Frenchie blow his top and go all-out in this war. That's what they want."

"And you're willing to go along with that?"

L'Heureux laughed again. "I told you, I'm for hire. But I had my own ideas. It seemed a shame to waste all that money just for a propaganda gesture. I had my own ideas, like I said. I'm going to keep that cash for myself."

"How many names do you know in the clique behind this scheme?"

"Practically all of them."

"Who are they?"

L'Heureux looked sidewise at him. "I'll write you a letter about it, chum, from South America. When I get there with the dough. Only trouble is, you won't be able to read it. You'll be dead. You'll be meat for the buzzards."

Chapter Fourteen

EACH STEP became an increasing torment for Jane. She was aware of muscles in her legs and body she had forgotten about long ago. Back in Texas, she had been considered reasonably athletic. She was good at tennis, she rode often, she never knew exhaustion. But for the last two months she had done little except sit passively in the heat and boredom of North Africa. There had been no tennis or riding in Marbruk. She had gone soft, but the lack of means to keep fit hadn't been the only reason for the way she had let herself go.

Every muscle in her legs was a tiny flame of torment. Dust burned in her throat. Her chest ached and there was an uncomfortable little cramp in her stomach. She knew she must look a perfect fright, with sweat running down her face, rivulets streaking through the dust that gritted her skin. A giggle lifted in her as she thought of what her friends at the country club would say if they could see her now. The giggle was silent at first, and then she heard the sound of it and it frightened her and she clamped her lips shut. Chet had looked quickly at her, glowering and yet alarmed.

Poor Chet.

He didn't know her at all. Not a bit. She was still a

stranger to him, even after the year of their marriage, even after the night of their reunion in Algiers.

Don't think about that night, she told herself. That's the cause of all your trouble.

She had almost told him about it this morning, but some perverse streak in her had checked her tongue. It was impossible now. Not after what had happened with Charley. Men were so stupidly jealous. And Chet was worse than most. He said he loved her, but he didn't trust her. He was only too willing to jump to the wrong conclusions about her. If he'd only listened to Daddy and kept the job in the Houston office, none of this would have happened. Everything would have been fine. But no, he had to come here to this god-forsaken, sun-blasted country peopled by maniacs, just to prove something to himself. It was only words, Jane told herself. This business of standing on his own two feet. Being independent. A man. Accepting no charity. Proving he could support her without help from Daddy.

It was all so sad and stupid.

She looked up and the horizon reeled drunkenly around her. How long had they been walking this time? She looked at the delicate Swiss watch on her wrist. It had stopped. Sand must have gotten into it somehow. Or the heat had expanded something inside. How long would it be before she stopped, too? She couldn't walk much more. She was thirsty again, too. The whole thing had been stupid. Why hadn't they stayed by the truck? The French soldiers would have come along sooner or later and rescued them. And why hadn't Durell been more careful about the driver? She knew the answer to that one, but her mind shied away from the responsibility. If she hadn't gone for that walk with Charley and even encouraged him to attack her, Durell wouldn't have left the truck to the mercy of Talek.

Well, she couldn't help that. She looked up again, seeing L'Heureux' tall figure striding along with his hands behind his back. They were traversing a narrow gully that paralleled the road. It was Chet's fault, really. She had tried to explain, but now he wouldn't listen. It just goes to show you. Charley could have escaped easily. He could have walked off as easy as pie. He might even have taken her with him as a sort of hostage. But he had thrown away his chance to escape because of her, because he couldn't wait to have her. . . .

102

The thought made a strange heat rise in her. He had just looked at her and wanted her. If he hadn't lost his head over her, he could have escaped. But he hadn't been able to control himself. She felt smug about that.

She wondered if Chet would have done the same.

No. Chet was too sensible. Too *prudish*. Even now, whenever Charley looked at her, it was plain to see that *he* hadn't given up. It was flattering to know she could do that to a man like Charley. A man who was dangerous, reckless, strong. If Chet didn't want her, she would certainly be all right, anyway. Besides, there was no real danger. L'Heureux was tied up again, and Durell seemed able to take care that he wouldn't step out of line again. It was too bad, in a way. But it was fun to know you had such power over a man, to know he was still a prisoner, maybe facing a death sentence, because he hadn't been able to resist her.

Suddenly Jane stumbled and fell. It came so unexpectedly that she was shocked and stunned. For several moments she didn't know what had happened. She felt herself falling and sliding, while stones and sand went roaring around her. Her cry was involuntary. The sun went spinning overhead, an awesome, blazing ball of fire that blinded her. Pain shot through her leg, and then there came a prompt repetition of that queasy feeling in the pit of her stomach.

Chet was beside her, kneeling. His tanned, square face looked young and concerned.

"Jane, Jane, honey. Are you okay?"

She looked at him blankly. "I fell."

"Let me help you up."

"No, I'm all right. Let me stay here a minute."

The others were walking, not running, back to where they waited. The highway was visible through a narrow cleft in the rock to her right. It shimmered like a wet ribbon in the sunlight. Jane caught her breath and rubbed her leg. It was all right, actually. She hadn't sprained or broken anything. It just hurt like the devil for the moment. She looked at Chet. She felt nausea rise like acid in her throat.

"You're awfully solicitous all of a sudden," she said.

"Jane, I've been thinking. Of course I was jealous. You and that man—I'm sure I was wrong in thinking you encouraged—"

"Oh, shut up," she said. "You're an idiot, Chet."

He looked as if she had slapped him.

Then she threw up.

It was awful. She had been fighting it for hours, and it was the first time Chet ever caught her at it. He had no idea what it meant.

She hadn't told him yet about the baby. And she wasn't going to, either.

Durell and Madeleine came up to her. Durell ordered Chet to move her into the shade of the tree and announced a second rest period. Madeleine knelt beside her. "Are you all right, *cherie?*"

The spasms were easing up. "Yes, thanks," Jane gasped.

The French girl's eyes were thoughtful, studying her. "Is it the heat?"

"I don't think so."

"Then this is not the thing you should be doing, *cherie.*"

"Please," she said. "It's nothing. I'm just tired."

Madeleine looked quickly at Chet. "If you wish it to be that way, of course."

"Yes, please. Maybe it is the heat, and the walking . . ."

"Naturally. But you must rest a little now."

"Only for a little time. A few moments."

"I understand, Mrs. Larkin."

But Jane didn't think the redheaded girl really understood. How could she? It was her own carelessness, her own thoughtless passion, that had brought her to this stupid state. Her mind went spinning back into the past, to the night two months ago when Chet had greeted her at the Maison Blanche airport outside of Algiers.

She remembered how it was that night only too well. She had really been looking forward to their reunion eagerly. She had missed Chet more than she had been willing to admit. And Algiers had looked like fun. It was like Paris and it was like San Francisco, with its terraces and hills and funny little streetcars and narrow streets and bright shops on the Rue d'Isly and the Rue Michelet. She remembered her first glimpse of the city as the plane had circled, the Sahel hills hugging the coast, lifting behind the buildings, so that the town looked suspended between mountain and sea. And the war didn't seem so terrible, with all the uniforms on the streets, the paratroopers in their cute green berets. . . .

There had been no restraint and no inhibitions in their reunion. They had gone directly to the hotel overlooking the semicircular harbor, and from the balcony they could look north at the darkening Mediterranean. They'd had a wonderful French dinner in the room, sharing a muted, breathless excitement every time they just looked at each other.

When she came out of the shower, she hadn't bothered to put on any clothes again. The room was filled with a kind of electric violet light, the dusky air was warm, the sea wind brought with it the tang of salt and all the exciting scents and strangeness of North Africa.

She remembered the look on Chet's face when she had walked toward him that way, with no clothes on. She had never done that before. His voice caught in his throat in such a funny way when he spoke her name. And then he took her with a crazy strength that was unusual to his gentle nature. Right there on the balcony, in the dusk, on the floor.

They had giggled crazily afterward. She accused him of raping her. But those heated moments had been repeated again and again that night, in an abandonment of mutual rediscovery.

The next day had brought quick disillusionment when they drove to Marbruk and Chet left her at Felix' hotel for a solid week while he worked at some emergency thing in the oil exploratory fields much farther to the south. By the time he returned, expecting a renewal of that night in the Algiers hotel, everything was different.

They hadn't slept together since. . . .

Chet's voice broke into her thoughts. "Jane, can you go on?"

Durell spoke above her. "She has to. Ten minutes are up. Everybody on their feet."

Chet said angrily, "Look, she's hurt her leg—"

"Then she'll have to be carried. We can't stay here. One way or the other, we go on."

"We can rest a little longer, can't we?"

"Not in this sun. Not here."

Jane hadn't heard that tone in Durell's voice before. It was like the crack of a whip. She stood up. Her leg was all right. It hurt a little, but not too much. She ached all over, but her stomach had settled down, thank God, and if things went according to schedule, she'd be all right for the rest of the day.

She looked at Charley L'Heureux. He was always watching, she thought. His eyes were inviting.

Why not? she thought. At least, he really wants me.

Chapter Fifteen

AT NOON, less than an hour later, Durell called a definite halt. It was too hot to go on, whatever the urgency. They ate dry sandwiches and sipped water sparingly, seated in the shade of huge boulders strewn on a slope above the Baroumi road. Not that the shade offered much relief. The landscape was scorched by the sun, shimmering with heat waves that distorted the vision and created crazy delusions wherever one looked. Durell allowed L'Heureux to join them while they ate.

The way ahead was over a long, flat stretch where no escape from the sun was possible. Moreover, Durell thought, their toiling progress would be visible to anyone for miles around. For that reason alone, it was impossible to go on. But it would have been murder for the two women, anyway. Of the two, Madeleine looked much better equipped for survival. She was sparing of any wasted motion, calm and withdrawn, as if her whole being was quietly concentrated on the simple problem of breathing the scorched air. Jane had deteriorated more than ever. She was limping now, too, and there was a pallor under her skin that indicated the near approach of exhaustion.

Chet kept his eyes on L'Heureux. He looked as if he wanted to kill the prisoner, the way he kept fingering his carbine. L'Heureux looked amused when he met Chet's hot, angry stare.

Durell had finished eating when he heard the distant sound of a motor. He stood up at once, holding his carbine ready, and studied the shattered landscape. To the northwest, where Baroumi was located, was a low range of brownish hills. Somewhere in the folds of the land close ahead was the village. Behind them was the twisted, rocky terrain they had just covered. Up to this moment, they had seen nothing living and heard nothing whatever of man.

The motor sound came from a plane. It came from the east, but it flew too far to the north for the pilot to spot them. The harsh sunlight flashed brilliantly on the yellow fusilage of the machine. It was an L-51, a light reconnaisance plane, and Durell wondered if it had flown in from the coast to Marbruk. If it had, his departure by truck might have been premature.

A dull thudding sound came from behind the low hills ahead. The plane circled in the sky over there. Smoke scarred the blue-white sky. It lifted in a black, greasy cloud, untouched by any wind.

L'Heureux stood up awkwardly because of the way his hands were tied, and walked over to join Durell.

"Baroumi is over there," the prisoner said. "I wonder what's going on. That's a French Army plane."

"We'll find out about it when we get there."

"Aren't you going to wait until dusk?"

"Yes," Durell said. "Sit down. And stay away from the girls."

Next he heard the sound of truck motors coming down from the hills to the north. There was more than one, but until they came into sight along the narrow road, he couldn't be sure. He counted three, then four, moving in a slow convoy. The figures of men trotted along after the slowly rolling vehicles. None of the men looked like French troops. There was too much lack of discipline in their movement. Durell swung back to L'Heureux again.

"What do you make of them?"

"You need help?" L'Heureux sneered. "You know damned well they're rebels."

Durell nodded. "If you make one sound to attract their attention, you're a dead man. Understand?"

"I thought you were supposed to take care of my hide," L'Heureux said, grinning.

"Don't count on it too much."

The trucks rolled closer. There was a sudden whining and thunder in the sky, and Durell saw the incredible flash of a fighter jet swooping up over the range of hills and then banking down over the convoy on the road. Rockets boomed and a louder explosion followed the drop of an antipersonnel bomb. One of the trucks careened crazily and went off the road and slammed headlong into a high outcropping of rock. Men spilled from it like shattered dolls. A few of them got up and ran for cover. The rest of the convoy had stopped. There was a small huddle of men who seemed to be tied together, and Durell lifted his field glasses to study the scene. The huddle of men were prisoners, mostly Arabs in robes and burnooses, although there were patchwork French Army uniforms among them.

The jet screamed overhead in a wide sweep and went back for another pass at the rebel convoy. Quick, repetitive noises came from its wing guns. Through the glasses, Durell saw spurts of rock and sand spout in regular patterns along the road into the parked trucks. Most of the guerrillas were already out of sight, hidden by rocky cover and ditches nearby. The truck that had crashed was burning now, sending a thick column of smoke straight up into the white sky.

The prisoners remained in a huddle like sheep in the middle of the road. Durell had no doubt they were being covered by the men hidden along the highway. They were caught helplessly between two fires, and it was impossible that the pilot of the jet could distinguish their predicament. The jet made one more sweep, and the prisoners went down like grass before the blade of a scythe. Durell lowered his glasses. There was a taste of acid in his mouth.

Chet Larkin stood beside him. "That was plain murder," he whispered.

Durell looked at the vanishing jet. "He didn't know that."

"Isn't there anything we can do?"

"Nothing, except stay here where they can't spot us." Durell looked at him quickly. Chet seemed to be little more than a boy. The shock of what he had just witnessed had made him pale. He said quietly, "The prisoners were Moslems, presumably loyal to the French. The rebels don't want any of that. They fight it with terror. If the jet didn't get those poor devils, the rebels would have had some amusement with them tonight before executing them. They don't have very pretty methods of torture. In a way, they were lucky to end the way they did. Quickly."

"Maybe we could make a rush for it and grab one of the trucks."

"There are about a hundred rebels down there. It's four hundred yards from here to the road, over a clear slope. We have just two carbines."

The jet was gone, screaming away to the north. It would be back in Algiers in a matter of minutes. The liaison plane showed as a glistening flash of yellow in the sky over the brown hills, and then that, too, vanished. The guerrilla troops straggled back to their trucks.

"Everybody up," Durell said. "Get behind these rocks. They'll be passing this way in a few minutes." He looked at the prisoner. "Remember what I told you, Charley."

L'Heureux looked angry for some reason. "You still going on to Baroumi?"

"Certainly. We've got to get to the bank, remember?"

L'Heureux lost his scowl and laughed.

The guerrilla *harkas* reassembled and rolled by their hiding place without incident. When they were gone, Durell left Chet to guard the prisoner and walked alone to the wrecked truck beside the road. It was still burning, and it was far beyond hope of salvage. The scattered bodies on the road had been left where they had fallen in the blazing sun. In a few minutes the place would not be pleasant. He looked up as a shadow flitted over him and saw the first of the turkey vultures in the white-hot sky. The rebels had picked up all the arms that had been strewn about. He picked up a grenade on one of the bodies and pocketed it, seeing it was of American manufacture. He wondered wryly by what devious channels it had reached this place and those dead hands.

He walked back to where the others rested in the shade of a small gully. L'Heureux was talking persistently to Madeleine in a low voice, although Chet was supposed to have kept him under gun point, away from the redheaded girl. Chet was arguing softly with Jane, and L'Heureux had taken the chance. Durell announced they would wait in this spot until just before dusk before going on to Baroumi.

Once more that afternoon the yellow liaison plane came circling over the brown hills, but it was too far away for them to attract its attention. And once, to the rear, a trick of terrain and wind brought them the irregular beat of gunfire somewhere.

Durell drank little of the brandy and a swallow or two of water and smoked the last of his cigarettes. He was accustomed to waiting. He knew that patience during the ordeal of boredom and waiting was a prime requisite in his business. He thought of Deirdre. He thought of Orrin Boston and Hadji el-Abri. Boston was gone now, fallen in the silent war, but someone else would inevitably take his place, because Orrie's job was still unfinished. It was only a straw, el-Abri said, perhaps of no significant weight. A small episode woven into the desperate pattern of vast and terrifying events. But he remembered the Kabyle's estimate of that straw. No man could say which straw would tip the delicate balance of events toward peace or toward war.

Durell did not regret being here. It was his job. He could not conceive of doing anything else.

At four o'clock Chet Larkin reached a decision. His throat still ached where L'Heureux had stabbed at him with that brutal judo cut. His head ached from the sun and the heat. His thirst was enormous, but he had taken no more water than Durell, turning the bulk of his share over to Jane. If things went wrong at Baroumi, they would be in real trouble, he thought. He knew that Durell was thinking about the rebel *harka* that had come this way, and he wondered what they had been up to. Then he decided it didn't matter. Right now he had to tell Jane what he had decided to do. He felt better about it now, having made up his mind once and for all. Back there in Marbruk he had made a mistake. He had been blind not to know that what he had told her was all wrong.

He got up and walked over to where Jane sat with her back against a dark red boulder. She looked tired, almost ill. There were deep shadows under her eyes, and her face still had that pallor of impending heat exhaustion. He could not read the expression in her eyes when she looked up at him and he sat down beside her.

"You keep watching him," he said.

"Who?"

"L'Heureux."

"Maybe he fascinates me," Jane said flatly.

He sighed. "Jane, this is silly."

"You're the one who's being silly. Over nothing at all. Absolutely nothing."

"You're lying," he said. "And you know it." He paused, trying to find a way to begin over again. It seemed impossible. During this day she had gone somewhere totally beyond his reach. She was like a different person, one he didn't know at all. Her eyes regarded him without seeming to see him. As if she were looking through him, and he wasn't really there for her to see.

She was like a sleepwalker, he thought, dazed by the heat, the exhaustion of their morning ordeal, by what she had seen happen on the road. "Jane, listen. Are you listening to me?"

"Of course I'm listening."

"Last night I was willing to do anything you asked.

110

Anything, you understand. I was ready to give up something I've worked for all my life. This chance to work out here on the geophysical teams is something I've always wanted to do. I wanted to be on my own, especially after the way things were all last year in Houston, living in your house. You know what I mean. Your house, your friends, your car. I don't ever want to be dependent on anyone like that."

"You really mean being dependent on my father, don't you?"

"Yes, I guess so. And on you, too."

"You never needed me, Chet."

"I didn't marry you for your money, if that's what you mean."

"I know that."

"But I do need you, Jane. I need you with me, beside me, helping me, maybe. I need to have the feeling that you and I are like—well, like one person. But it isn't that way, and it never will be that way. I thought maybe there could be a compromise. But everything has to be the way you want it. Soft and easy. Have fun and drink and run around with the country club crowd and let your father do the work."

Jane turned her head slowly to look at him. "What are you trying to say, Chet? We've been over all that. You're exaggerating things and you know it. I just want what I think is best for us. I'm not a child. And I'm not a fool. I know what the world is like. Tomorrow we can all be ashes. Why not enjoy what we can get today?"

"Jane, listen—"

"I don't know what you're talking about. You're always castigating yourself about imaginary things. Like those Middle Ages monks who wore hair shirts and tormented themselves for their ideals. But this is the twentieth century and there's death in the air for all of us."

"That doesn't mean a man has to stop and just fold his hands and wait to die because some maniac might push a button on the other side of the world, Jane. Don't you see, we can't play and have fun every day of our lives because it *might* happen. I thought last night I was ready to give in and do things your way. But I've been thinking about going back—you know, to Texas, and all that—I've been thinking about it all day."

"There's nothing to think about," she said coldly. "We'll go back, if we ever get out of this."

"No, Jane," he said. "You're wrong. I'll get you to Algiers, somehow. I promise you that. But I won't go on that plane with you."

Her eyes were simply blank. "What does that mean?"

"If you insist on going home, I can't stop you. But I wish you wouldn't. I wish you would stay here with me, where my job and my work is. I only want you here with me as my wife, Jane. I love you. You know that. But if you insist on leaving me, I can't go with you."

"Are you deserting me?" she whispered.

"It's the other way around, isn't it?"

"You know how I hate this place."

"But it won't be forever, Jane. Don't you see that? Maybe just another year—"

"A year!"

"—and there's a future here for me, a reputation to build in the field I want to work in for the rest of my life. I can't give it up."

"And I can't stay," she said flatly. "Not now, especially not now." She wasn't going to tell Chet about the baby. Not ever, as far as she was concerned. She felt betrayed. She had been so sure of Chet. But he was different now. She searched his face, looking for any sign of the change in him. She didn't understand him at all.

"You don't love me any more, is that it?" she said slowly.

"You know that's silly. You know I do."

"Just because I went with Charley and he got nasty—"

"No, not because of him. Not at all."

"Yes, it is," she insisted. "That's what made you change. You think I'm a tramp, just because he tried to get funny with me, a man like that, who's been in prison so long—"

"Jane, please—"

She got up and walked away from him.

He didn't go after her.

He was through with chasing after her, he told himself.

They reached Baroumi just before sunset and waited in a small ravine in the hills for the desert dusk to deepen. The road into the Arab village was empty. Nobody moved in the *douar*.

A few stunted pines grew in the ravine, with ragged grass cropping out on the stony slopes. In the village itself, some date palms showed their plump yellow-green tops above the *mechtas*. Durell left the others in the ravine and walked forward with the carbine and field glasses to the top of the slope, where he could look down on a barley field and another grove of date palms and a vineyard into the market place.

The shadows were long and deceptive. A hot wind blew from the arid south, shaking the shaggy palms. He saw nothing. Nothing moved. There was no sound. Nobody walked in the market place. Smoke curled lazily from a burned-out hut nearby, and the barley in the field looked as if it had been trampled by a company of running men.

Durell's mouth tightened as he swept the small settlement with his field glasses. Baroumi looked utterly deserted. Then something moved at last, slinking in the shadows of an alley off the market place. He saw it was a dog. The dog was dragging something out of sight. He kept watching. The dog was a thin, ribby mongrel, hauling his morsel out of the alley to settle down beside it. It was the body of a Moslem woman, dressed in a torn and dusty black gown, her veil off, her lanky black hair dragging in the dust. He turned the glasses elsewhere. Now he saw the pockmarks of bullets scarring the houses and more evidence of fire and looting.

But surely, he thought, somebody had been left alive in the *douar*.

He saw nothing in motion except the dog.

There was a communal well in the market place, and to the left was a second collection of houses indicating another spring. Glass suddenly glittered in reflection of the setting sun, and he adjusted the focus of his lenses. It was a red Ford truck of ancient vintage. It stood alone behind one of the houses that seemed larger than the rest. It didn't look damaged. It simply seemed to be abandoned.

Looking down at the village, he had the feeling he had seen all this before. Especially the house with the truck behind it.

He studied the road twisting into the northern hills toward the coast. Nothing moved except a dozen buzzards picking at things that lay in the roadside ditches. Then the wind shifted, and Durell smelled the town, and in the wind were the odors of charred wood, and of death.

He turned and went back to his party. Chet was covering L'Heureux with his carbine.

"There's a truck in the village," Durell said. "It may not have any gas in it, and it may not work at all, but it's the only one I can see. There's nothing else."

"Can we go down there?" Madeleine asked.

"There doesn't seem to be anything to stop us." Durell looked grim. "I don't think there's anyone left alive."

Madeleine touched her throat. "Was it the raid?"

"They were all killed or taken prisoner by the extremists."

"Why the extremists? Why not the French? Or el-Abri?"

"Baroumi was el-Abri's home. It was his *douar*," Durell said. "I was here before, a long time ago. Years ago. His parents lived here, and el-Abri took me to visit them." He turned to Chet. "Can you hold things quiet here for half an hour?"

"Are you going in alone?" Chet asked.

"I'll take Madeleine with me," Durell said.

"I don't want to see what's down there," the girl said quickly.

"Maybe you'd better. Just to see what Charley's friends can do."

Her face was pale. Then she shrugged. Durell turned to where L'Heureux had settled down, sitting on the rocky ground. The big blond man looked disinterested.

"Which well has the money in it?" Durell asked.

"I'd have to show you, chum," L'Heureux said. "And why should I?"

"I'll convince you later," Durell said.

He started off with Madeleine down the scrubby slope toward the village. Long shadows reached ahead of them, and the sky to the west was suddenly aflame with brilliant color from a distant sandstorm. To the east, the first stars shone in the purpling sky.

They crossed the barley field and passed several burned-out *mechtas*. In front of one hut was a man, sprawled in death. A dead woman and a child lay to one side of the road. A grenade had caught them. Durell said nothing. Madeleine turned her head and looked the other way.

Nobody challenged them except a bony dog that came whining up and lay down on its belly and looked at them with yellow eyes. The silence of death hung over

114

the village of Baroumi. The shadows thickened into solid dusk as they reached the market place Durell had studied with his field glasses. No one was here. There were several more Arab bodies, men and women killed indiscriminately in blood-lust. There seemed to be no vehicles other than the one Ford truck he had spotted from the hillside. The village itself was small, with a population of not more than two hundred people, and of the two hundred, not one remained in the vicinity. Those who were lucky enough to escape the massacre had taken to the hills for good, Durell thought.

"Your friends are thoroughly efficient," he said quietly.

Madeleine's voice was small. She had tied back her long red hair with a white ribbon. There was dust on her arms. The open collar of her blouse showed smooth, tawny skin down between her breasts. Her reply was almost inaudible. "They are not my friends, Durell."

"Yours or Charley's—it's all the same. Do you know their names?"

"It is not the same. Not any more."

"Do you know who they are?" he asked again. "Those men in Paris and Algiers, and those in the councils of the rebels—they are all alike. They want this to go on."

"I don't know who they are. But they are not my friends."

"Do you still expect me to believe in your change of heart?"

"I don't expect you to believe anything," she said. "You are a hard man. I have been watching you all day. I don't think I like you, Durell. You frighten me a little. You think of only one thing. Nothing else is important but your job."

"In which well did Charley hide the money?"

"I don't know that."

"This is not the time to hold back on me, Madeleine."

"I told you, I don't know."

The dog with the yellow eyes had followed them from the road, and now it was joined by three or four more—ghostly, skeletal figures that whined and padded in their tracks through the thickening darkness. Durell turned decisively away from the market place when he saw that the communal well here had been destroyed by a grenade that had caved in its walls. He went down a small alley. There was a house at the end of the alley, surrounded by a high wall, with a wooden gate in the

115

wall. The gate had been blown away and the wall was scarred by bullets. Durell led the redheaded girl through.

Nothing ever changes much in the desert, he thought. The passage of time had left few marks that hadn't been erased or smoothed by the shifting winds until it all looked the same again. How long had it been since el-Abri had taken him here? More years than he cared to remember. This quiet house, this date palm leaning over the roof, were all well remembered. It might have been yesterday. He had hidden here with el-Abri for over a week, because the Vichy C.I. people had gotten wind of their radio transmissions with the Algerian *maquis* before the North African landings. He had eaten, slept, fought, and laughed with the Kabyle people here. He remembered el-Abri's father, a tall man whose memories went back to the savage wars against the Foreign Legion. He was an old man even then, like a dark oak in dignity and strength. El-Abri's mother had hidden behind the ways of ancient tradition, and he had rarely gotten more than a glimpse of her. She had existed as a soft, sliding footstep, a suspected smile behind a black veil.

Nothing had changed. Yet everything was different.

"What place is this?" Madeleine whispered.

"El-Abri was born here," Durell said.

"You know it well?"

"Yes."

"But no one is here now."

He didn't reply. He walked around the house to the walled garden in the back. He found the bodies there.

The old man had been tortured. The old woman had been stripped and defiled. Probably the mother had been killed first, in an attempt to make the old man talk to the rebels about where el-Abri could be found. The extremists considered el-Abri a traitor. Durell was sure that neither one had yielded anything about their son.

The body of the old man hung by his feet from the limbs of a gnarled olive tree that had been ancient when Durell was here before. The thickening shadows made the scene grotesque, distorting it, adding a macabre touch to the heavy silence that oozed from every corner of the walled garden.

He heard Madeleine being sick behind him. He turned back to her

"Please. I want to go," she whispered. "Why did you take me here?"

116

"I had to know what happened," he said.

"You're too cruel. It's not my fault these people were killed."

"You helped it to happen," he said.

She was shivering. "Let's go back. Can we go back now?"

"Not yet. We'll look at that truck first."

But the truck was a disappointment. It had been too much to hope for, really. It was not far from the el-Abri house. Through the glasses it had looked intact, but when he walked up to it he saw that a grenade had thoroughly wrecked it, and that was why it had been abandoned here in this dead village.

They were no better off than they had been that morning.

Worse, probably.

Chapter Sixteen

IT WAS DARK when Durell returned to the others in the hills. A cool wind blew over the barren slopes, and the moon made distorted shadows in every direction. The dogs kept following them, whining, and when Durell ordered the others to come back to the village with him, the dogs padded after them.

Chet walked beside Durell. "You say everybody was killed or taken prisoner?"

"It looks that way."

"And the truck is no good?"

"We still have only our feet to travel on."

"Can we make it back to Marbruk?"

Durell looked at the two girls. "I doubt it."

"Then I don't see what we can do," Chet said. He scowled at the moonlight. "If the rebels worked according to pattern, they've also ruined the water supply here. There won't be any food or water and no transportation. The telephone lines are cut. It's a dead end."

"Not quite," Durell said. "The French were in on the action here. You saw the jet yourself. They know what happened here."

"Are you suggesting we stick around this charnel house until they show up in force?" Chet lifted his carbine dubiously. "Seems like better odds the rebels will come snooping back to collect any odds and ends before the Army makes it."

"That's a possibility," Durell admitted.

"And the rebels will collect us, too."

"We'll take that chance," Durell said. "It all depends on which side gets here first. We know that DeGrasse is short-handed in Marbruk. He may not be able to spare a detachment from his garrison, or he may not care to take the risk. The situation is unusual, with the extremists so bold—or so desperate—in this area." Durell thought about the money and decided that could well be the cause of it all. He added, "But what happened in this village is something the French will want to investigate and publicize. It's too important to disregard. I'm betting the French get here first. And the thing for us to do is to sit it out for them."

"I don't think Jane can stand much more," Chet said.

"She can take another day of it. One way or another, it won't take longer than that."

"I'm sorry about what happened with her and your prisoner."

"Nothing happened," Durell said sharply. "You ought to realize that."

"I know, but still—" Chet looked at L'Heureux' big, arrogant figure, then at his wife, walking with Madeleine. Both girls were talking in French. Jane's French was halting, but she knew enough to make herself understood.

"Everything has gone wrong between us, you know," Chet said to Durell. "It's a mess all around. I guess your own plans are plenty fouled up, too. We should have been in Algiers by now. If it wasn't for that *goumier* driver ratting out on us, we'd be all right."

"Just be grateful he didn't cut us down with his tommy gun."

One of the dogs trailing after them began to growl suddenly. The sound was low and alarming in the dusk. Chet broke his stride and halted abruptly. His chunky body was tense and frozen as he lifted his carbine. Nothing moved in the shadowy market place except the dogs. L'Heureux, several steps ahead of the others, sat down on the edge of the community well in the middle of the square. The girls halted, too. In the moonlight, the village might have been asleep rather than murdered.

The dog growled again. Chet snicked back the bolt of his carbine. "Who is it?" he called loudly. "Who's there?"

118

There was no answer. L'Heureux laughed thickly. "You jumpy, Chet, boy? You don't know what war is like, do you? Too young for the big one, even too young for Korea, huh? You're nervous, huh?"

"Somebody is out there," Chet insisted. "Out there in the dark." He looked frightened in the shadowy starlight. "I heard something. And look at the dogs."

There came a heart-stopping beat of huge wings and an awkward, gorged shape lifted from one of the dark doorways. The dogs barked like maniacs. Durell looked up and saw the soaring wingspread of an African turkey buzzard.

"Keep your shirt on," he said. "And put down your gun."

"This place is the worst I've ever seen." Chet wiped the flat of his hand across his mouth. The cool desert breeze suddenly made his trousers flap loudly around his ankles. "I still think it was a man back there."

"It might have been," Durell said.

Chet looked sharply at him. "Did you see him?"

"No, I didn't see anything."

Chet blew air out from his lips. "This place is like a berserk butcher shop. We just can't expect the girls to stay here."

"Let's see first if L'Heureux was telling the truth about his cache of money."

Chet looked angry. "This is a hell of a time to be thinking about money."

"It's important," Durell said quietly.

"You'd do better to put a bullet through that bastard's head instead of protecting him."

"I may have to do just that," Durell said.

L'Heureux looked indolent and at ease as Durell walked over to him. The man had no intention of running off into the shadows of the village now. He preferred to remain with them rather than risk being caught by returning rebels or blood-crazed survivors, with his hands tied behind his back. Durell looked at the well in the market place.

"Is this where you hid the money?"

"Hell, no," L'Heureux said. "You don't think I could've slipped in here in the middle of all these gooks, do you?" He shrugged awkwardly and jerked his head. "It's a little way down that street. You going down the shaft after it?"

119

"Why not?" Durell asked.

"It's tricky. I'd hate to see you lost *and* the money, too." L'Heureux laughed thickly. "Maybe we ought to have chow first and refill our water bottles."

"Not from this well," Durell said. He leaned over the stone parapet. "It's been stuffed with a few dead bodies."

L'Heureux moved off ahead. The street was narrow, with small houses hidden behind walled gardens. A gutter ran down the center of the walk. Durell kept his gun ready. He couldn't shake off an uneasy feeling about this dead village. He watched the windows and doorways carefully, but nothing stirred. He heard only the crunching of their boots and the dry rattling of palm fronds in the trees overhead.

"Down here," L'Heureux said.

They were only two houses from el-Abri's. A small communal well stood in a recess beyond a primitive Moorish arch. Several water jars lay in broken shards on the sun-baked bricks around the well.

Durell leaned over and looked down. Starshine led his vision down the ancient, mossy brick sides. He smelled cordite and the acridity of a recent explosion. He could not see the water. He heard a faint trickling, but it sounded muffled, as if it were forced through debris. He backed off and found a stone and dropped it into the well, trying to estimate the depth before it struck bottom. The stone did not strike water. There came a miniature echoing, like a tiny landslide down the shaft. Twenty feet. Perhaps thirty.

"Somebody dropped a grenade down here for good luck," he announced. "The well is ready to cave in at any minute."

L'Heureux showed alarm for the first time. "Hell, you've got to go down! There's a fortune waiting for me down there!"

Durell had been thinking about the problem. He didn't want to trust Chet on guard here while he lowered himself into the shaft. Nor could he ask Chet to take the risk of going down.

"Let me go down," L'Heureux said urgently. He strained at the bonds that tied his hands behind his back, and his shoulder muscles writhed under his tattered shirt. "What have you got to lose? We need the water, anyway. How long do you think we can hold out when the sun comes up tomorrow? You might have to take to the hills again, if the rebels come back first. You'll need the water."

"You're too anxious to get down there," Durell said.

"Hell, I don't care who goes down. Let Chet do it."

"No," Jane said suddenly. "Not Chet." Chet looked up, surprised. Jane went on, "I can do without the water. Really, I can."

"But you can't," Durell decided. He gave Jane his carbine to hold. "Can you use this?"

"Yes, I've done skeet shooting—"

"Cover the prisoner. You, too, Chet." Durell cut L'Heureux' bonds with a pocket knife. "Go ahead, Charley. And bring some water back up with you."

"Sure thing."

L'Heureux straddled the stone coping around the well and sat there for a moment, rubbing circulation back into his big hands. He looked at Madeleine and grinned as she turned away. Durell took his carbine back from Jane. The interior of the well shaft was of rough stones, and the diameter was not too wide to prevent L'Heureux from bracing hands and shoulders against one side and finding toe holds on the other.

He edged down into the deep hole.

It was a piece of cake, Charley thought. He hadn't figured on some idiot rebel dropping a grenade down the well, but even that had worked out. Otherwise, Durell might have sent Chet down.

His hands were still numb and tingling from the long hours of having them tied behind his back, and his shoulders ached from muscular strain. He let himself down carefully, feeling the roughness of the stones against his back, gripping the adjacent stones on either side with his hands flat beside him and digging with his toes against the cracks and crevices on the opposite wall.

He looked up and saw the circle of night sky overhead, the shining stars, the dark oval of Durell's head. He hoped Madeleine knew that this was the big thing. He couldn't see her or the Larkins. Just Durell, watching.

"It's cold down here," he called up.

"Make it quick. Let me know when to lower the canteen."

121

"I don't see any water."

"You can hear it, can't you?"

His voice echoed curiously with a note of thunder reverberating from the stone walls of the shaft. Charley lowered himself a few more feet. He tried to remember how it had been when he left the money here. How far down was it? He smelled the still-lingering fumes of cordite from the grenade that had blown in the bottom of the well. The stupid bastards, he thought. If the money had been destroyed or buried—

But it couldn't be. He had put it, tin box and all, on a shelf just above the water level. It ought to show up soon.

He touched bottom sooner than he expected.

There was no shelf. And no water level. Only rubble, a mass of razor-sharp stone chips and sand trickling away from where he braced his foot. Charley got his weight adjusted on the pile of stone. The whole thing might collapse under him and bury him here, and he knew there would be no help from Durell if he was trapped like that. He began to sweat. He told himself to take it easy, measure every move, disturb nothing until he was sure of where he was and what he was doing. He wished he had a flashlight. But only Durell had a torch, and he hadn't obliged by passing it down to him.

"Hey," he called.

"Are you ready for the canteen?" Durell asked.

"Sure. Pass it down."

There was no water. He could hear it trickling somewhere in a cavity under the rubble he stood upon, but it might as well have been running into China, for all the good it did them. He didn't intend to dig down and risk getting trapped down here just for them. He could stand being without water better than the rest.

But where was the money?

The shelf where he had hidden the box was gone. The whole place was unfamiliar. When he was here before, there had been a rope and pulley and hand grips down into the shaft. The grenade had changed all that. But the tin box had to be here. Somewhere. Under the rubble. It couldn't be too far down.

He began to move the stones away carefully, sensing the hollow under him that waited only for a shift of balance to drop him with a couple of tons of rock and sand into the true bottom of the well. He sweated even

122

more, despite the clammy cold. He felt around in the darkness. His hands had lost their numbness. But he could not find the ledge.

"L'Heureux!"

He looked up. He saw Durell's head and the muzzle of his carbine over the edge of the well.

"I'm all right," he called.

"I'm passing down the canteen."

"Fine."

He saw the steel bottle in its khaki case lowering on a length of rope that had been used to bind him. He waited for it and when it came down he untied it and placed it on the rocks at his feet.

He had it figured out now. The explosion of the grenade had caved in the ledge and slid out a long slab of sandstone that was jammed against the opposite side of the shaft. He could feel the tilt of it plainly now. He removed some of the smaller stones and felt the water-smooth ledge. It was only eight inches wide. He shifted carefully, to stand on it. There came a rumbling and a grinding noise underfoot and the mass of debris carrying his weight suddenly dropped a few inches. He stood very still. His heart hammered crazily.

"L'Heureux!" Durell called again.

"I'm stuck."

"How bad is it?"

"Give me a few minutes."

That would hold him, Charley thought. He moved some more stones and suddenly his fingers felt the sharp edge of metal. A great flood of relief swept over him. He tried to pull the box loose. It wouldn't move. He began to curse and sweat. The sandstone slab pinned the box to the ledge. He tried to lift it. There was no purchase, and he did not dare exert too much pressure or the whole business would cave in. He tried again. He got his right hand under the edge of the sandstone slab and his left on the small corner of the tin box. He lifted again. Nothing happened. Once more. The box moved an inch or two and then again, and he felt a darkness surge over his brain with the blood-crushing effort. From high above came the distorted echo of Durell's voice, calling down to him. He thought he heard Madeleine, too. He didn't look up.

Once more.

The box came free.

One end had been partly crushed and flattened, and the lock was sprung so the lid was twisted partially open. He felt inside. The money was there.

And the gun.

Charley opened the box all the way and felt the wads of currency and pushed them aside until he got a grip on the heavy Colt .45. He turned his head then, his big shoulders hunched, and looked up at the circle of starlit sky above. He could see Durell leaning down, and Madeleine and the Larkin girl, too. But they couldn't see him. It was too dark down here for that. He took the Colt and slid out the magazine, and by his sense of touch he checked the heavy slugs in their copper jackets. Then he slid the magazine back into the butt and forced the barrel back until a shell went snicking into the chamber and the hammer was cocked.

He laughed silently. He tugged at the canteen dangling on the end of the line. "Hey, Durell! There's no water! I can't reach it and I ain't going to try. Pull the can back."

"I can hear the water running," Durell called down.

"Yeah, but I can't reach it. I'm coming up now."

"Use the line, then."

"Hell, I don't need it."

Charley straightened and thrust the Colt into the belt of his khaki slacks. He would need both hands to make the climb back up.

"Did you find the money?" Durell called.

"Yeah, I got it."

"Tie the box—did you say it was in a box?"

"Yeah, a tin box."

"Tie it to the canteen. We'll lift that first."

Charley pretended to hesitate. "How do I know you won't just clobber me and drop me back in here, huh?"

"You know better than that. You and I have a date in Paris," Durell said.

Charley's laughter filled the well shaft with wheezing, whispering silence. "Okay, pal, I trust you. Just don't run off with the loot, huh?"

He tied the tin box and the canteen to the line and watched it rise in swift, swooping jerks to the top of the well and vanish into Durell's hands. The moment Durell's head was withdrawn, to examine the contents of the box, as Charley guessed might happen, Charley jumped for a hand hold on the wall of the shaft, got one leg

124

braced against the opposite curve, heaved with his muscular shoulders and gained another foot, stopped for an instant to get his hands flattened against the stones below and behind him, and then surged up in a twisting, rising, spinning leap that brought him within three feet of the top of the well. His right hand shot up and outward, his fingers caught at the coping stone above, clawed for a moment, and held. His body thudded hard against the well wall as he dangled there for a moment by one hand. He jerked convulsively, got his other shoulder up, his other arm up, his left hand on the coping. A moment later he heaved once more, his shoulder muscles cracking and straining to lift his weight, and then his head came above the top of the well and he was out of it like a dark, giant cat.

The first shot went by his head like a thunderclap.

Jane screamed. The second burst of shots chipped stone from the edge of the well in a harsh spray that stung one side of his face.

He didn't know what was happening. He could see the moonlit market place clearly, after the darkness of the well. Durell was to his left. He held the tin box in his left hand, his carbine in his right. Durell wasn't the one who had fired at him. Nor had Chet. Chet had stumbled and fallen to his knees, and Chet's carbine lay in the dust in front of him.

He couldn't understand it.

He pulled the pistol from his belt, snaked over the well coping, and dropped flat on the ground. The third burst of automatic fire went over his head.

Charley saw it now. He was the target. It was one of those crazy things you couldn't count on. One of those things not even Durell could anticipate.

Somebody was shooting at them from the alleyway nearby. It was where the dog had sensed something earlier and had shown it by his growls. The man was a dimly defined shadow under the leaning walls of a yellow house. He seemed to be on his knees. Then Charley saw the glint of moonlight on the barrel of a tommy gun and a sudden spray of bullets went hammering and screaming again in their direction. It was wild and crazy. It made no sense.

The man with the tommy gun began cursing in a high, thin voice. He was yelling something in Arabic, and Charley heard his own name, shockingly, in the middle of the incoherent stream of hatred. Durell shouted to the man to drop his gun. The echoes of the tommy gun were enormous in the silent, dead village. The man's screaming incantations were the voice of a pain-crazed lunatic shouting at the cold Sahara moon.

Charley raised himself and leveled the Colt and fired one shot carefully at the Arab's shadow in the alley. The screaming curses ended. The man dropped. Durell yelled at the same time and Charley twisted, still on his belly. He saw Chet leveling his carbine and fired again. The bullet hit Chet in the shoulder and knocked him into the dust around the well. Chet tried to get up and Charley fired again. He missed. It didn't matter. He reached with his left hand, lunging upward for two steps, and his long arm went around Jane's waist. She had been standing as if paralyzed for all these moments. He dragged her body flat against his and swung her around to face as he did, toward Durell.

"Now," Charley gasped hoarsely.

Durell had dropped the money box. He was holding his left hand with his right. His carbine had fallen. A thin trickle of blood came from Durell's clenched hand.

Durell looked at Charley's gun and nodded curiously. "All right, Charley."

Charley was a prisoner no more.

"Please . . ." Jane moaned. She sounded out of her mind with terror. "Oh, please, stop it, stop it, don't shoot any more. . . ."

"Take it easy, baby."

"You shot Chet—"

"He wasn't much, anyway." Charley looked at Durell. "Stand away from your gun, huh? Mad, pick it up. Use it on him if you have to."

Madeleine got up and nodded. Her face was pale and blank. She moved like a sleepwalker toward Durell and picked up the carbine. Charley couldn't tell what she was thinking. He didn't quite trust her. He watched her until she stepped back and faced Durell and covered him with the carbine.

Charley let out his breath in an explosive laugh. "You got creased, Durell? The gook nicked you?"

"In the hand," Durell said quietly. "Where did you get the pistol?"

"It was with the money. I had a hunch I might need

126

it the day I picked it up. No telling who I'd be with."

"I thought it was something like that," Durell said. "I was ready for you, Charley. You ought to know I was ready to kill you as you came out of the well."

Charley laughed again. "But the gook threw you off. My break, huh? The way the ball bounces. It's happened with me before like that." Charley felt breathless. There was a great pressure of exultation squeezing in his chest. He enjoyed holding Jane's soft body close to him. He could feel the trembling warmth of her flesh against his thigh. He could smell the womanliness of her. He knew he was hurting her, crushing her in the grip of his big arm. He didn't care. He squeezed her harder.

"Let's go look at the gook," he said.

Nobody moved. Chet groaned, sprawled in the dust. Charley kicked Chet's gun away. He sharpened his voice.

"Move, Durell. Now I'm the one who gives out orders."

Chapter Seventeen

THE ARAB in the alleyway was Talek. Durell turned him over at Charley's command and saw that Charley's single shot had caught the *goumier* in the mouth and burst open the back of his head. Charley took the tommy gun and Durell's .38 and the single grenade Durell had picked up on the road. He went back to the well and dropped the .38 into it and Chet's carbine. That left Charley with the Colt and the tommy gun, and the grenade. Madeleine had Durell's carbine.

Durell took a handkerchief from his pocket and wrapped it around his wounded hand. It was just a crease, a burn across the knuckles, from one of Talek's wild, stray bullets. He ignored the pain. He had been nicked just at the moment when he could have dropped Charley. He tried to fight down the angry frustration he felt. There was nothing he could have done to make things work out any other way. A bad break, that's all it was. Bad enough to wreck everything he had planned. Bad enough to get them all killed by this renegade who laughed and waved his Colt around.

He forced his mind to reconstruct what must have happened. He was sure now that Talek, the truck driver, was one of el-Abri's men. He had sabotaged the truck and deserted them in the hope of contacting el-Abri so that the Kabyle chieftain could pick them up in the desert. Probably el-Abri had planned things that way. But the Kabyle's plans had gone awry, too. He hadn't anticipated the extremists' raid on Baroumi. The extremists were as much el-Abri's enemies as the French.

All right, Durell thought. So Talek took off for Baroumi. He went to el-Abri's house here and got caught in the rebel raid. Somehow Talek survived, hid out until now. He looked at the dead *goumier*. Charley's bullet wasn't his only wound. One arm had been shredded by a grenade and there was blood on the man's uniform from a bullet in his stomach. Talek must have been out of his mind with pain and weakness. But not too far gone to realize what was happening when he saw them at the well. Talek had been shooting at Charley, no one else. But in his condition, he had done the worst possible thing.

He looked at L'Heureux. The man still held on to Jane.

"Let me go," Jane moaned. "Please, please . . . Chet is dying. . . ."

"Not much of a loss, baby," Charley said.

"Please. Let me help him."

Charley saw Madeleine looking at him in a peculiar way. He let Jane go. When he released her, she sagged and fell to her knees, and her blond hair fell across her tormented face. Then she pulled herself up and ran to where Chet still sprawled on the ground beside the well.

Durell said, "He's been hit in the shoulder. But I don't think any bones are broken."

Jane scarcely heard him. She knelt beside Chet and gently lifted his head. There was a great soaking stain of blood running down his left side. He was breathing strangely. All at once a wild fury took her and she lunged crazily at L'Heureux, hammering at him with her fists. L'Heureux slapped her. His hand was hard and explosive against her cheek. She fell to the ground in front of him and began to sob.

"I'll let you help him," Charley said. "But you can't work against me, too. One or the other, take your choice."

Durell said, "What do you have in mind?"

"You want to know right away if I'm going to kill you?" Charley weighed the tommy gun in his hand and pretended to consider it. "What do I need you for?" He looked at Madeleine. "You with me, Mad?"

"I always have been, Charley."

"You bet," Charley said. "Pick up the money, Mad."

She did as he ordered. Durell stood in a quiet attitude of listening. After the slamming round of shots, the stillness of the night clung to the dead village. Several dogs had barked for a minute or two in wild hysteria, but nothing else happened. There was no one left in Baroumi to care.

Madeleine stood beside Charley in the quiet, whispering night. The wind was cold. On the ground nearby, Jane sat with Chet's head resting on her lap. Her face was agonized as she appealed to Durell.

"Can't you help me? Won't anybody help?"

L'Heureux shrugged. "Go ahead, Durell. Just to settle your mind, I can use all of you. Alive, I mean. So long as you hop when I tell you to hop. Understood?" He paused. Nobody spoke. "All right, then. I want the boy scout walking in fifteen minutes, or we leave him."

"You wouldn't," Jane breathed.

"Don't tempt me, baby. You and I got a date later on."

"You're a monster," she whispered.

He grinned down at her. "The kind you like, huh, Janey?"

He looked enormous, his broad shoulders and round head pushed forward as he grinned in the starlight. Durell watched and waited. It was difficult to guess what L'Heureux planned to do. His hand throbbed painfully as he helped Jane tear a bandage from her blouse and make a crude compress for Chet's shoulder. Durell's brandy flask brought the boy around somewhat. He groaned and rocked his head from side to side.

L'Heureux picked up the length of rope and handed it to Madeleine. "Tie up Durell here. He gets a taste of his own medicine. See how he likes hiking with his hands behind his back."

"I thought we were going to stay here and wait for the rebels." Durell said carefully.

"Odds against it they get here first. The paratroopers will drop in by morning. No, we're getting out."

"On foot?"

L'Heureux grinned. "You're nosy, huh? I'll tell you anyway, Durell. I got a jeep, a radio, and water hidden in the hills. We go up there."

Durell gestured at the Larkins. "You don't need them. Why not leave them for the French? They'll be better off."

"I can use them both. In different ways, though. But you be careful, Durell. You stay alive as long as I can use you, not a minute more. The minute you pull something, you're out, you're meat for the dogs. The only reason I keep you is for an insurance premium, see, against the French. And if we run into my pals in the rebels, they'll be happy to have you and point to you as a foreign agent interfering with internal affairs here." Charley rubbed the back of his hand across his mouth. He seemed consumed by a poorly suppressed excitement. "Of course, you know I don't want to meet anybody. Mad and me are getting out with the loot. To hell with making propaganda with a quarter of a million bucks. If I make it, you can all walk home any way you like. But if you make trouble, you're dead. Got it?"

Chet was on his feet. In the starlight, his face looked ravaged. He leaned heavily on the two girls. Charley picked up the money box. The night wind made his cropped yellow hair look like a silver hood closely fitting his round head.

"Tie up Durell, Mad," he said. "If the boy scout can't make it, we'll drop him on the road."

"I'll make it," Chet said thinly.

They started out again. Durell walked ahead. Madeleine had tied the knots around his wrists with surprising strength, and his fingers were growing numb. But the bullet crease had stopped bleeding. L'Heureux had gotten grim satisfaction out of Durell's discomfort.

"You kept me like that long enough, buddy boy. Now it's your turn. Just follow the road into the hills. I'll tell you where to turn off."

The wind blew sand along the village streets, and the palm fronds clacked dryly. A bit of newspaper blew across the shuttered shop fronts. The moon was already setting. Durell's mind was on the Larkins. Jane was in bad shape, and he didn't think Chet would make it far. A .45 slug puts any man down for a long time, even if it's only a flesh wound. He didn't see how Chet could keep up with them for any distance.

He heard light footsteps behind him and Madeleine

130

fell into step. The village, with its smells of death and desolation, was behind them. The road lifted into the barren foothills ahead.

"Be careful," Durell said at once. "Your Charley won't like you to walk with me—unless he gave you permission."

"He doesn't care. He's very sure of himself."

"And you?"

"I don't know what to think."

"You sided with him when it mattered," Durell said.

"He had the gun. You were hurt. One does not argue with a gun, anyway. I have seen him like this before. He would shoot you down without a thought. One obeys a man like that when he gives orders."

"How is Chet doing?" Durell asked.

"A little stronger. He refuses help. He drives his wife from his side. He is a stupid young man, I think. Can't he see what Charley wants? That Jane is blind, too. She doesn't know the man Charley can be."

"What happens when we get to this place where Charley expects to find his jeep?" Durell asked.

Madeleine shrugged. "He will probably kill us."

"If the jeep is there?"

"Especially if it is there. He won't need us then."

"You include yourself among the victims, I notice."

"He is tired of me. He looks only at the blond one, that Jane. All day it has been like that with him. Can you explain what makes a man obsessed like that?"

Durell walked on for a moment. "Madeleine, did you know about the gun he had hidden in the well?"

"No."

"You knew about the money, though."

She shrugged again. "It was a dream. A wonderful illusion."

"You don't think he'll take you with him, if things work out as he hopes?"

"Not any more. He will take the Larkin girl. For part of the way, anyway." She kicked at a pebble on the road. "His ego is so great, he can't conceive of any woman turning against him. It is difficult, at that. I saw him in a situation like this once before. Something happens to him. Perhaps he becomes truly himself, without restraint. Like a clever madman. He will give orders, simple ones at first, then those that are only devised to humiliate and debase you. For the moment, he enjoys having us at his feet, but in the end he will simply shoot us."

"You seem quite sure he'll kill you, too. Will you help me, then?"

"That is why I walk with you now."

"We've got to get the gun away from him," Durell said.

"You are a man of directness. First things first, eh?"

"Can you do it?" Durell asked.

"You mean, can I get near enough to him tonight to steal the weapons? No. He will not have me. He will take Jane, instead."

"But if you tried—"

"He will reject me," she said flatly.

"Then if you can tell Jane what must be done—"

"I already have. She understands. She has agreed. She will try to get Charley's weapons and if she succeeds, she will kill him."

"No," Durell said quickly. "He's my prisoner, still. He must be brought back to Paris to talk about this matter."

Madeleine looked grim. "Jane will not succeed, anyway. She is too soft, too spoiled. Charley will take her and use her and laugh at her afterward. She will try, but she will fail."

"Is there anything else you can do?" Durell asked.

"No."

"Then Jane has to try," he said.

He didn't like it. He had never subscribed to the use of women in this business, although it was an accepted commonplace in many instances. He told himself he had got rid of any false notions of chivalry. There was no chivalry in this war. It was mean, gut-twisting, back-knifing struggle, with no holds barred, no rules. You did what you could and you used whatever weapons came to hand, or you died.

The wadi entrance ahead was a narrow cleft in the rock, not important enough to attract attention from the road, but wide enough to permit a jeep to drive in. Charley ordered them into the starlit gloom and after a few steps the walls of the ravine widened and then turned abruptly to the right. Durell halted, and Charley pushed him on angrily.

"You first, buddy boy."

"Do you expect to meet anybody here?"

Charley breathed hard. "You never know with these gooks."

"I don't see any jeep."

"You don't see the cave either, do you? It was an arms cache for the rebels a couple months ago, but they gave it up, don't ask me why. They're always going off half-cocked, like a bunch of bloody amateurs. So I had the jeep cached here, along with a radio."

Durell went around the sharp bend in the wadi. A flat face of limestone loomed ahead and he looked to right and left into the angular shadows of the ravine, but he saw no other way out. The forty-foot cliffs formed a natural cul-de-sac. To the left was a fault in the layers of stone, where one huge slab overlapped another, the ragged edge slanting up at a sharp angle. If you looked at it casually, you wouldn't see the gap behind the outer fold of rock, the triangular opening that led into the face of the cliff.

"Mad!" L'Heureux called. "Go get the jeep out."

Madeleine vanished quickly into the dark slot between the stones. Durell looked at the Larkins. Jane had eased Chet to a sitting position against a boulder, and Durell, looking at the wounded man, decided that Chet Larkin was tougher than he looked.

Madeleine came out of the cave almost at once.

"Charley, there's no jeep in there."

"What?"

"The cave is empty."

"Mad, don't joke with me—"

"I'm not, Charley, it isn't there!" She sounded desperate.

L'Heureux grabbed the carbine from her hands. He now had all the weapons in the group, Durell noted. The Colt .45 was jammed in his belt, the first carbine was slung by its shoulder strap, along with the tommy gun, and the grenade was crammed into the left-hand pocket of his ragged khaki pants.

"The jeep's got to be there, Mad. Is it a trick? Something you cooked up with Durell? You expect me to go in there first?" L'Heureux suddenly smashed his knuckles across the girl's face. Madeleine fell, sprawling, her hair across her eyes. "That's for trying anything at all, see? Now get in there and drive that jeep out."

She didn't get up. She shook her head.

"Mad, I'm warning you!"

Durell said quietly: "It's possible she's telling the truth. Maybe the jeep *isn't* there. You said yourself this place was used by the rebels. Maybe they came back and found the jeep and drove it away." In the dim starlight, he saw

Charley's figure as something enormous and glowering. He could hear the man's harsh breathing. Durell walked over to Madeleine. He couldn't help her up; his hands were tied behind his back; but he dropped to his knees beside her. "Tell him again. Tell him the jeep is gone."

Charley cursed. "All right. Nobody moves. I go in there and if anybody moves a finger, they get it, understand?"

Madeleine whispered, "He means it. Be careful."

Charley went into the cave. Nobody moved.

When he came out again, Durell saw by his face that Madeleine had told the truth. The jeep Charley had been counting on wasn't there. Charley, for all his careful planning, was trapped along with them.

Charley stared at them and licked his lips. The starlight glistened in his narrowed eyes. "So it's gone," he announced. He looked at Durell. "But don't get any ideas. There's still a radio in there. I'm calling the rebels, and we'll sit tight until they pick us up here."

"What happens to us then?" Durell asked.

"Whatever they want. You'll make a great hostage for them. Good propaganda, being an American agent."

"Do they know about the money?"

"No," Charley said. "And they won't know, either."

They looked at each other.

"Suppose one of us mentions it when they get here?" Durell asked. "You can't watch us all. And the minute you took off alone, we could talk. They'd be on your heels before you got very far."

"So?"

"So don't lie to us," Durell said. "You have to kill us before they get here."

"Don't push it," Charley said. "Don't push it now."

Madeleine whispered, "Please, Charley. No more right now. Please."

"He wants me to knock him off," L'Heureux said heavily.

"You know he didn't mean it that way."

"Then let him ask me to save him for a few hours." Charley walked across the gritty sand and put the muzzle of his carbine against Durell's head. Durell could smell the oil on the gun. He still knelt beside Madeleine. The huge shape of his former prisoner loomed over him. Charley said, "Go ahead, beg for it, you son of a bitch."

"Let it go, Charley," Madeleine whispered.

"Shut up and stay out of it. Well, Durell?"

134

"No man wants to die," Durell said carefully.

"That ain't enough."

Durell saw Jane and Chet staring at him. They seemed to be holding their breath. Then L'Heureux laughed explosively.

"Funny thing, Durell. I got a gun at your head and I can kill you now and get away with it. No reason why I shouldn't. But you can't kill me. You wouldn't, even if you had the chance."

"Don't count on that, Charley."

"I don't. But in your mind, I'm still your prisoner. Your hands are tied, my gun is on you, but you still think I'm your prisoner, right?"

"Maybe."

"No maybes. I know your kind. I know the training they give you. You never give up, you bastards. You got orders to take me back to Paris so the French cops can pick me apart and then hand all the bloody little pieces back to you so you can take me to Washington where they'd do it all over again. Those are your orders. That's what you hope to do. So you wouldn't kill me, even if you had the chance."

Charley took the gun away. The muzzle scraped Durell's head with a harsh twist and then was lowered to point at the black sand.

Chapter Eighteen

THEY ATE the last of the sandwiches. Jane refused to eat and gave her portion to Chet. Madeleine sat down with Durell and helped him with his, since he was still tied. He had hoped, faintly, that Charley might permit his wrists to be unbound, but Charley had ignored the problem. He was worried, too, about his wounded hand. The pain in it had become a steady, pulsing throb that reached up into his arm, and he mentioned it to Madeleine when she asked him how it was.

"It can be changed," she murmured. She looked at the mouth of the cave, where Charley had vanished briefly with Durell's remaining brandy. "It will be dangerous. You saw how he was when he found the jeep was gone? He could have killed us all without a qualm."

"He's quiet enough now."

"Because he has made contact by radio with the rebels. The radio was there, in the cave. I saw it. Charley has already sent off his message. He feels secure now. He thinks his friends in the extremists will come and bring a vehicle for him."

"When does he expect this to happen?" Durell asked.

The girl shrugged. "He will not say. It is difficult to guess. Here, finish this last bite."

She gave him the last of her sandwich. There was no water left in the thermos jug now. Durell knew that if the rebels didn't come soon, the sun tomorrow would finish them all. He kept watching the cave entrance where Charley had gone and said quietly, "Can't you untie me now, Madeleine?"

She was combing her hair. "It would be suicide, and I will not help you with that. Not now. He has all the weapons and he is alert. When he finishes your brandy, he will not get very drunk, but he will relax a little and then he will send for Jane Larkin."

"Or you," Durell said.

"No, it is the blond girl from Texas he wants, not me."

"And then?"

"He is like a bull, that type. It will be quick. We will not have much time, only a few minutes. I will untie you then."

"When will it begin?"

"When he finishes the brandy." Madeleine's blouse was torn, and her shoulder gleamed through the ripped cloth. Her eyes were luminous in the starlit ravine. It was very quiet. Durell swept the rim of rock where they waited, but nothing stirred. He heard Jane murmuring to Chet, where they sat a little apart. She was holding his face in her hands, talking quietly and persistently to him. All he could see of Chet was the gleam of crude bandage on his shoulder. His head looked bowed and stubborn, as if he refused to listen to her.

Then Charley appeared in the black mouth of the cave. He threw something, and glass shattered. It was the empty brandy bottle. His legs were apart, his head was thrust forward on his massive shoulders. Everything in his black silhouette reflected ugly suspicion.

He turned at last to Jane Larkin.

She hadn't told Chet, and he had no idea that the night in Algiers would have a lasting meaning for them both. She prayed now that nothing would happen to make things go wrong. It didn't matter right now that Chet was remote, removed from her by a barrier of pain and his stubborn decision to stay in North Africa. Maybe he was right. She had reached a willingness to concede this much. No question about it, she had been a bitch. It took something fundamental, like seeing Chet shot and falling, seeing his blood and his tired face, thinking for a heart-stopping moment that he'd been killed. Then you knew what really mattered and what was trivial. She wished she really knew how to pray. She tried, but it seemed as if she had forgotten, or didn't know how. The words ran through her mind without conviction or meaning. Maybe it was too late for her.

"There he is, Jane," Chet whispered. "Watching you."

She didn't look at the cave. "Give me your knife, Chet."

"Too late now, honey."

"He can't see. It's too dark. Where is it? You said you had one."

"Jane, you can't kill him!"

"I've got to try," she said quietly. "You heard Durell. If the guerrillas get here, he has to kill us so we won't tell about the money."

"Then why doesn't he do it now and get it over with?"

"He wants me," she said flatly. Chet looked at her. His face was haggard. She touched his cheek, and his beard felt rough and stubbly. "But part of his wanting me won't be satisfied unless you and Durell and Madeleine know he has had me. That's the kind of man he is."

"How do you know about that? What do you know about men like Charley L'Heureux?"

"I just know," she said. "That's how he is."

Chet started to speak in violent protest, then paused, swallowed, and looked at her in wonderment. "And afterward?"

"Afterward, he'll kill us. Me, too. I have no illusions about that." She listened to the sound of her whispered words and it seemed like the calm conversation of a stranger. It was not the way she felt inside. There were storms of confusion and terror in her. But for Chet's sake, she had to seem calm. "There won't be any afterward, though. So hurry and give me your knife."

"He's gone back inside," Chet said, looking at the cave.

"Hurry, then. Where is it? You said you had it."

"In my boot."

He tried to get it for her, but his shoulder wound had stiffened him, and he groaned involuntarily with the effort. Jane told him to lie still. The knife was in his left boot, in a small leather pocket made for it. It was a spring knife, with a long bone handle and a small silver button at one end. She pressed it experimentally. The blade snicked quivering into sight, long and thin, glistening in the starlight. She touched the point. It was like a needle. She touched the edge of the blade with her thumb. It was very sharp.

She tried to imagine driving this blade into Charley's flesh. She couldn't picture it. It was an event that didn't exist. But she had to make it happen.

She got to her knees and knelt beside Chet.

"Jane, I can't let you do it!" He sounded desperate.

She kissed him. "Don't worry about me." His face was in the shadow. She could see the agony of his love and fear for her. "Chet, I'm sorry about all the—all the quarreling, you know—"

"Don't talk about that now."

"I wish I could forget it. I've been terrible to you."

"I've been no saint, either."

"Yes. Yes, you are a saint, Chet. Later, if everything works out all right—" She swallowed over the words that didn't say what she was thinking. "Well, we'll talk about it later, all right?"

"Sure," Chet said.

She kissed him. His beard scratched her, She stood up quickly and closed the knife and unbuttoned the bottom button of her blouse and slid the knife against the skin of her stomach. The touch of it made her muscles jump and contract.

Charley's voice reached for her in the night.

"Jane? Come here, Jane."

She looked that way, pretending indecision. "What do you want?"

"Come here, Janey."

She walked up the rough slope to the cave entrance. None of them since their arrival had been near the cave. Her legs trembled as she climbed toward him. She prayed for the strength to do what had to be done. Smile, she told herself. Play it the way you did all day. Play it as if you were still the idiot you were this morning. Smile

138

again. Now. And when he touched you, don't flinch. Whatever you do, make him think you like it.

"Here I am," she said. She pretended to be interested in the cave. "What's in there?"

"Nothing. I had a jeep, and somebody swiped it. Good thing they left the radio."

"Charley. . . ."

"Yeah, Janey."

"It's kind of hard for me to figure out what's right and wrong." She made her voice naïve and plaintive. Her belly quivered. "I mean, things have happened, everything is so crazy and unreal—"

"I'm real." He grinned down at her and put his hands on her shoulders. "I know what you've been thinkin' all day. Same as me. We both knew it, the minute you first saw me. I know you, Janey."

"You make me feel—sort of funny," she said. She looked down and put her arm across her belt and felt the hard pressure of the knife. She heard his breathing. She could smell the sweat and animal-odor of him. His fingers caught in the open throat of her blouse and she heard the buttons tear, one by one, as he slowly pulled his hand down and ripped the blouse open.

"Don't," she whispered. "Not here. They can see—let's go inside—"

"They don't count, Janey. Forget them."

He ripped the blouse away. She felt the night air on her body. It had to be now. Her forearm hid the knife, and she dropped her hand with the knife lying in her palm and then she suddenly felt the brutal pressure of his arms as he pulled her to him and kissed her. His mouth was hard and cruel. His strength was enormous. She couldn't move. Her arms were pinned to her sides by his embrace. All at once she was terrified. She felt him crush her down. She hit him, breaking free for a moment, in an instinctive effort to resist. Her fist was small and puny. He laughed. He threw her down, and as she fell she pressed the button on the knife handle, and the blade sprang out with a tiny snicking sound.

He heard it and was motionless.

Straddling her, his silhouette was enormous.

"Janey," he said reproachfully.

Jane lunged, driving the knife upward toward his body. And she knew before the stroke went half the distance that she had missed.

His knees came down, crashing on her upper arms, and his hand flicked aside the blade with astonishing ease. His face hung over her, laughing silently. His head and shoulders blotted out the sky. Everything seemed to stop inside her. She felt his weight on her and then the shock of his desire.

She heard a curious cry from Chet down below in the ravine.

She screamed.

Charley rolled and stood in a crouch beside her, waiting. Chet came struggling up the slope to the cave. His face was dark with anguish.

"Come on, boy scout," Charley whispered.

It was quick and efficient. Chet's wild attack was doomed by his wound, his weakness, his blind rage. It was easy for Charley. Charley let him swing and ducked and laughed, and then he stabbed a hard left into Chet's belly and followed that with a knee lift that smashed into Chet's face and slammed him backward. Chet went down. He rolled over twice, down the slope. His arms and legs seemed boneless, flapping with the roll of his body. His head struck a stone with a flat sound and he lay still, like a discarded pile of ragged clothes, dim and motionless in the starlight.

Charley turned back to Jane.

She had fainted.

He didn't care.

Durell felt rage move in him and break all the cool and calculating moves his training required. It didn't matter now. Jane's move hadn't worked—it had been disastrous. He knew that this was the time to be calm, to let what was happening up there go on. He couldn't let it happen. He couldn't stay down here and let Charley do what he was doing.

"Get me loose," he whispered harshly.

Madeleine trembled as she untied the knots binding his wrists. "The animal," she whispered. "I don't want to look at him up there with her. Like an animal in the field. But he knows I will watch. It is part of the amusement and pleasure for him."

"Hurry it up," Durell said.

"I think he killed Chet."

"Killing comes easy for Charley. Did you see where he put the guns?"

"Just inside the cave entrance."

140

"But he's got the pistol with him, right?"

"And the grenade."

Durell's hands came free, He moved his arms a little. He looked up at the cave. The two figures up there were locked together as one. He stood up. He kept his hands behind his back, as if they were still tied. There are so many ways to kill a man, Durell thought. Simple, easy ways. You don't need a knife or a gun. A pebble would do. A rolled-up newspaper. Orrie Boston had told him that one. A stiffened finger, stabbing and rupturing. He could do it. He wanted to do it.

Madeleine put her hand on his arm as he moved to take the first step up there. "No, wait. He will only kill you, too."

"I can get up there fast," Durell said.

"But you will not try to kill him, will you?"

"I have to bring him in alive and talking."

"But he has no such inhibitions." Madeleine was angry and impatient. "Oh, don't you see? We are both angry. And shocked. And that poor girl up there—with her husband dead—"

"We don't know Chet is dead."

"And we don't dare go to see if he needs help, do we?"

"I'm going," Durell said.

She held him back again. "Wait." She breathed quickly. She faced away from the cave entrance. "He will kill you. I know him. He is waiting for you now. After the husband, then you. It is his way of pleasure. It is what he planned, you see. Now he is waiting for you."

"He's busy," Durell said cruelly.

"Not so busy that he doesn't know we are here talking and wondering. He does this deliberately, don't you see?"

Durell looked down at her. She looked small and slight, no longer the elegant Parisienne model. He almost liked her. But she was right. He couldn't kill L'Heureux.

"And your hand?" Madeleine said. "How is your wounded hand?"

He had forgotten about it. Now that she had cut the bonds on his wrists, the circulation was restored. He looked down at his fingers. There was blood on them. There was a long scar on the back of his left hand, and it was bleeding again, and when he flexed his fingers and made a fist, he felt the pain go all the way up his arm into his shoulder.

"Let me go up," Madeleine said urgently. "He is expecting you, so I will go. I can get one of his guns. He won't stop me, you see. That type will be amused. I have heard stories about his habits with girls. More than one girl. The thought will come to his head when I walk up there. He will think I want—he will be diverted, you understand."

"No, I can't let you go first."

"It will distract him. Are you so angry you are blind? I thought you knew your business better than this. You think you shouldn't send me, a woman, first? We will all die if we do not win. I am going. You can't stop me."

"Madeleine—"

She turned from his grip and walked quickly up the slope, almost running, before he could stop her. The wind blew her hair across her cheek. Durell watched her walk through a pattern of silver moonlight and dark shadow. He cursed, started after her, checked himself. If he followed now, while Charley watched, they would both be killed.

A few pebbles rolled with surprising noise from under Madeleine's shoes. She came to the long shapeless mass of Chet Larkin's body. She heard him breathing, though he didn't move when she paused beside him. But he was still alive. Maybe he would die soon, in a few minutes. There wasn't time to look at him to see if she could help.

She walked on toward the cave.

Charley was sitting up. Jane lay on her stomach with her face in her arms. Charley looked at her and smiled strangely.

"Mad? Come to see the fun?"

"Charley, you're too cruel," she said.

"Come on up, Mad."

"I'm coming, Charley. What's the matter with Jane?"

"She's a sensitive type. She passed out, right away."

Charley's voice was thick with something that went beyond anger. He looked irritated, sitting with his legs crossed tailor-fashion, beside the unconscious girl. The cave was a wide, dark crevice behind him. She wanted to turn her head to see if Durell was following, but she didn't dare move Charley's attention that way. Had he started yet? She couldn't be sure. She walked all the way to where Charley sat. His close-cropped, yellow hair looked white in the starlight. His face looked shapeless and slack, as if the bones had dissolved in acid cruelty.

142

She had never seen him like that before. She tasted hatred and enjoyed it.

His voice stopped her as if he had slapped her.

"You untied Durell, didn't you, Mad?"

"What?"

"You cut him loose. You're on his side now, right?"

"Charley, listen to me—"

"And here he comes," Charley said.

He stood up all in one movement, with swift, fluid grace. Madeleine tried to stop him when he took the Colt from his belt. She thought he was going to fire at Durell. She could hear Durell's steps running behind her, crunching on the rough wadi floor. Then she saw Charley turn his head as if his neck was stiff and she saw he was pointing the gun at her. He was smiling queerly. She heard the crash. She felt the bullet hit her with incredible, tearing strength.

Then she was on the ground, conscious of being on her side, with a great numbness inside her body. There was no pain. She looked up and saw Charley standing over her. He still smiled. It was the same look he'd had on his face the first time he had taken her. He pointed the gun at her again, and she saw everything very clearly, all the mistakes she had made, all the little cruelties and vicious lies she had helped him with, and she knew that this had been the biggest mistake of all. She saw his knuckles move on the trigger of the gun and just before the gun fired again, she knew that he had killed her.

And then she knew nothing any more.

Chapter Nineteen

DURELL kept running at the second shot. His anger pushed him forward, one step after another. He didn't care about his orders now. He wanted to kill L'Heureux. If Charley let him get five steps nearer, he could do it.

"Hold it," Charley said thickly. The gun swung toward him.

Durell stopped. "Is she dead?"

"She's dead."

"She was your girl."

"You can have her now," Charley said.

Madeleine looked like a child's doll tossed idly aside

and discarded. Her eyes were wide and staring. They caught the starlight with an illusion of life. Durell swallowed. His anger refused to subside. He couldn't control it. His life depended on this control, but he couldn't find it. He couldn't do it.

He took two more steps toward the man who straddled the earth like a behemoth atop a mound of his victims.

"You've done quite a bit tonight, Charley. You ought to be proud of yourself. You've cleaned us out."

"Not quite," Charley said. "You're still around."

Durell could not see his face. The moon had gone down below the upper edge of the wadi, although long slabs of its pale light still slanted into the far corners of the ravine. Charley's face was a dark wedge turned toward him, a black outline against the pale luminosity of the sandstone behind him.

Durell thought he heard sand run hissing into the wadi somewhere to the rear. He heard a stone fall, rattling, bouncing, clinking. Charley heard it, too. Neither man moved. They both listened. There was the wind. The stars were silent. There was nothing more to hear.

Durell knew he couldn't go back now. And Charley's gun kept him from going forward. Three steps away. He remembered how it had been at the Maryland farm, where Orrie Boston had been an instructor. He remembered it all, the techniques for assault, for murder. But Charley L'Heureux knew these techniques too. Charley would be good at them. He had to be good, to win against Orrie, who had already become suspicious of him.

"Go back and sit down, Durell," Charley said. His voice rang harshly in the night. "I've got the money, I've got the guns. The rebels will be here soon."

"When they come, you'll kill me, too," Durell said flatly. "You'll have to, because of the money."

"Maybe you'll be reasonable."

"I don't seem to have anything to lose," he said.

He made his move when Chet Larkin groaned and stirred. The sound caught Charley's ear as Durell drove up toward him. There was no stopping now. Durell came in low under the big man, and he heard Charley suck in his breath an instant before he twisted aside. The gun crashed. The report was thunderous against the dark sandstone walls of the wadi. The sound of it blotted out Charley's yell as Durell hit him. Durell's shoulder smashed just above Charley's knees. He felt

144

the gun club his back with wild, massive strength. Charley went over backward. His knee clipped Durell's chest and then they both slid and slipped and rolled down the dark slope to the bottom of the ravine.

Durell's first aim was simply to hang on. He could not let Charley get separated from him, because then Charley's gun would come into play again. But his grip on Charley's wrist was only a fragile hold. He managed to cling to it while they rolled over and over down the slope. Charley's weight was plunging, thrashing, punishing. They slammed into a boulder, and a grunt of pain came from the big man, and Durell flipped his weight against the thick wrist, smashing it against the stone. The gun fell free. Sand went hissing out from under their straining bodies, and they slid in a small avalanche to the very bottom of the wadi.

The gun was gone, lost in the sand.

The dim starlight failed to light the darkness here. With the gun out of the way, Durell rolled aside and got his legs under him and lifted himself to a crouch. There was little to see. The dark walls of the ravine rose in smothering heights to right and left. The sand embankment down which they had tumbled from the cave entrance was behind him. Charley stood with his hands held away from his sides, his shoulders hunched stiffly forward. He was a faceless dark mass, and Durell could smell the man's sweat and hear his thick, controlled breathing, and that was all.

"Come on," Charley said. His whisper was ragged. "Come on, Durell."

"Give it up," Durell said. "There's no place to go."

"I finished them up there. I got the money. There's only you. Come on, come closer."

"We're not alone," Durell said.

"What?"

"They're watching us."

"What?"

"From the top of the cliff. There, off to the left. There's starlight on a rifle barrel."

Charley's laughter bubbled in his chest. "I wasn't born yesterday, Durell. That's an amateur trick."

"No trick," Durell said. "Look at him up there."

Charley's head moved fractionally. The glint of reflected starlight was no longer there. A cool wind blew down the narrow length of the wadi, and sand suddenly came in a stinging eddy behind Durell's back, blowing toward his enemy. It went into Charley's eyes, but Durell didn't move. He knew that if he closed with Charley now, he wouldn't stop until Charley was dead. Or until Charley killed him. His anger was too violent, born of what had happened to Orrie Boston, the Larkins, and Madeleine. He was afraid of what was happening to him because of his anger, but he couldn't help it. Charley dashed sand from his eyes and took a step backward and Durell stood where he was. Charley sounded puzzled, speaking through the windy darkness.

"You could've taken me."

"Why bother? We're both in a bottle and the cork is tapped in tight."

"I don't see anything," Charley said.

Sand hissed around their feet. Charley backed up another step. His shoulders touched a huge boulder and he jumped, turned his head quickly to scan the sandstone cliffs around them, then turned back to Durell.

Durell's anger was beginning to ebb. "They're all around us," he said. "Watching us."

"The rebels?"

"Maybe. Call out to them and see," Durell suggested.

Charley was silent. His breathing was ragged. Only his eyes flashed white in the dark mask of his face. Durell knew he could take him now. The gun was gone, lost in the sand. Charley had changed. Something had put fear into him. But it was not the fear of a weak man. It made him all the more dangerous at the moment.

Still, there had been an imperceptible shift in the man, and Durell took advantage of it. He closed the gap fast, his body slamming Charley back against the boulder. Charley hit him in the stomach, tried to knee him, hit him again with a sledge-hammer right. Durell took the blows and returned them. He slashed at Charley's throat, missed the point he sought, and slashed again. Charley screamed. He tried to escape. He slid sidewise to get away from the rock at his back. Durell didn't let him go. He struck again and Charley made a queer coughing sound, kicked at Durell, and caught Durell on the thigh. Durell spun away, came back again. He saw Charley's ravaged face. It was the face of his enemy. The face of Orrin Boston's murderer. He didn't want to stop now. He struck again and again. His left hand was bleeding. He felt the pain all the way to his shoulder and down his side. He did not spare himself.

Charley went to his knees.

He was strangling.

"Don't kill him, Durell," someone said.

Durell stopped. He was trembling. His anger shook and churned in his belly. He kept watching Charley and didn't turn around to see who had spoken. Charley was trying to crawl away. The man's huge body looked curiously flattened and crushed. His hands scrabbled at the gravelly soil. His big head with the curiously blond-silver crop of hair hung down from his massive, muscular shoulders. His breathing was queer, like a wounded animal's.

"Durell," someone said again.

Durell turned. It was Hadji el-Abri.

The Kabyle guerrilla and his men seemed to have sprung up all around them like ghosts conjured out of the moonlight. El-Abri stood tall and straight, a tommy gun in his hands, pointed at Durell and Charley. His men stood in a circle just beyond. Their faces were the faces of the wind and the desert.

"Save him for me, Durell," el-Abri said quietly.

Durell looked at the Kabyle. "How long were you watching?"

"A few minutes. You knew I was here?"

"I was expecting you. I know Talek must have sent you a radio signal about us. Talek was your man, right? It couldn't have been anyone but you."

El-Abri looked around the wadi. "What about the others with you?"

"I don't know. They need attention."

"I have a medical officer with me." The Kabyle gave swift orders in Arabic. One of the armed men in ragged khaki nodded and went up the slope toward the cave entrance where Madeleine's body lay. Durell watched him for a moment. He saw the Arab doctor look at Madeleine and then turn away with a shrug and help Jane Larkin to her feet. Jane ran, stumbling, to Chet. The doctor knelt and began doing something to Chet's shoulder. Durell looked back at el-Abri.

"Are we enemies?" he asked the Kabyle quietly.

"The choice was yours."

"L'Heureux is still my prisoner. I still claim him."

"Not any more. He belongs to me, now." El-Abri issued another quiet order. One of the men stepped

147

forward and gave Durell a drink of brackish water from his canteen. Durell sat down on the sand. His hand was bleeding heavily. He tore a strip from his shirt and bound it roughly. He was still shaking. He looked at el-Abri's face and saw no friendship there. No help at all. It had all been for nothing, he thought. All the nightmare of the last twenty-four hours, the struggle to get away from here, might never have been.

He got up and walked through the circle of guerrillas. Nobody stopped him. He went up to the cave entrance, beyond Madeleine's body, and picked up the box of currency and walked back again.

He looked at Charley. Charley sat on the sand, hugging his knees, his head lowered. He had the mark of death upon him.

Chapter Twenty

MADELEINE was buried before they moved out. Durell noted a quick tension among the guerrillas, a wariness in the way they moved, as if they expected to be trapped in this place. Even el-Abri showed his impatience with the delay. But the grave was dug and Madeleine's body placed in it and covered over with the stones and sand of the desert.

"She was L'Heureux' woman," el-Abri said quietly. He watched the grave-diggers work. "But I notice he does not look at her for a last time."

"He's the one who killed her," Durell said.

"Yes, we heard the shot. We were searching the area for you. Why did he shoot her?"

"Because in the end she chose my side."

"You speak of her as if she was your friend."

"I think she was," Durell said. "But I couldn't save her."

He turned away, a flat emptiness in him. There was something he wanted to do, but he could not think what it was. Perhaps he was too tired, too filled with pain. He thought he owed something to Madeleine, and he looked at Charley, searching for it.

Charley lifted his head and looked at him from under coarse black brows. "Are you going to let these gooks kill me, Durell?"

148

"Why not?" You hold life cheap, don't you?"

"Look, take me back to Paris with you, huh?"

"It's not up to me any more."

"You know what el-Abri will do to me? These gooks are worse than the wild Indians ever used to be. They've got ways of torture—"

Durell turned his back on the man's rising terror and walked away.

It was only a short distance to where el-Abri's trucks were hidden. The night was cold, and the wind blew sand viciously in their faces. Two of el-Abri's men made an improvised litter and put Chet Larkin on it. The doctor walked on one side of the litter and Jane walked on the other. Jane seemed unaware of anything that was happening except in the immediate circle of her husband, and Durell did not interfere with her.

He spoke only briefly to the doctor. "Will the young man live?"

"It is in the hands of Allah. But he should be in a hospital."

"Can we do anything for him now?"

"I have given him morphine for his pain and sulfa for infection. It is the best I can do with what we have."

"Just keep him alive," Durell said. He looked at Jane and spoke to her. "Chet will be all righ . Don't worry."

She didn't pay any attention to him.

There were two trucks hidden in a narrow fold of the low hills. Durell could see the highway to Baroumi where they got into the trucks. On one side of the road was a vineyard, trampled and destroyed, the vines cut down to the ground. He looked at his watch to see what time it was, but his watch had stopped. He only knew it must be some hours after midnight. It didn't matter, he decided.

El-Abri had a scout car of World War II vintage with the troop trucks. A radio antenna whipped in the rear, and the driver looked no more than sixteen. The Kabyle motioned Durell into the hard back seat and joined him, lifted his arm in a signal, and the small convoy moved off, bouncing across, the ruined vineyard toward the highway. They used no lights. In the deserted hills, enough radiance came from the wilderness of starlit sky to let them guide their way.

"You're going to Baroumi?" Durell asked suddenly.

"Do you remember it, Durell?"

149

"From the old days, yes, when you and I hid there, with your people, from the Vichy police."

"I have a few things to do there. And I must pick up Talek at my father's house."

Durell looked at the Kabyle. "Haven't you been to Baroumi tonight?"

"Not yet. I will satisfy myself there with Charles L'Heureux' death. Then I will let you go, Durell, you and your American friends, the Larkins. I will see to it that you are found quickly by the French, before the sun gets too high. You will be in Algiers in time for lunch. I think that is fair enough, my friend."

Durell started to speak, then was silent.

"Is something wrong?" el-Abri asked.

"You won't find Talek in Baroumi. Talek is dead."

"Dead? You killed—"

"Not I. Not L'Heureux, either, although his bullet was the last to enter Talek's body. It was the rebels." Durell spoke bluntly, his voice harsh. "The extremists raided Baroumi yesterday afternoon. I thought you would know."

"I have been far to the south. You are sure of what you say? You do not try to confuse me—" The Kabyle's lean face was like stone. "What happened there? You were in the village tonight?"

"We were there. That is where L'Heureux hid the money box you now have. We saw the end of the extremists' raid and waited until dark before we dared to go in." Durell paused. "You know how the extremists operate, especially the terrorists. They are as bad as those of the French who lean toward fascist terror in a hope to end this war. They are equally evil."

"You use words to prepare me for what I am afraid to hear." The Kabyle's face was still, his whisper almost inaudible. "Did you see my parents there, Durell?"

"I saw what the extremists did to them," Durell said gently. "They are dead. I am sorry, old friend."

The Kabyle sat without moving in the back of the jouncing scout car. They were rolling swiftly along the road, curving up into the hills again, retracing the long, exhausting walk they had made during the day. The barley fields came into sight. The wind whipped el-Abri's short khaki jacket. No sound came to him for a long minute.

"I am sorry," Durell said again.

"But they were innocent," el-Abri whispered. "They were old and they were innocent."

"Yes."

"Was it—was it bad for them?"

"Very bad," Durell said.

"You do not spare me anything, do you?"

"You will see for yourself."

Nothing was changed in the *douar*. What had taken Durell half a day to cover on foot was only a matter of minutes in el-Abri's convoy. The village looked the same. There were only thirty men in el-Abri's patrol, and they fell silent as they looked at the death and destruction around them. El-Abri stopped the young driver of the scout car at the narrow street where his father's *mechta* loomed beyond the garden wall. He said nothing more to Durell. He went ahead alone.

Durell got out of the car. Nobody stopped him. He walked back to the truck where the Larkins were. Chet was on his stretcher on the floor of the truck, and Jane sat beside him, her eyes anxious.

"How is he?" Durell asked.

"I don't know. He's still unconscious."

"El-Abri promised to deliver you both to Algiers in a few hours. Chet will be all right, I'm sure," Durell said.

Jane made a swallowing sound. "Can't we go there right away?"

"I'm afraid not. There's still some unfinished business to take care of."

She lifted her head. "L'Heureux?"

"El-Abri is going to execute him—the hard way."

She shuddered. "I don't want to see it."

"Then stay in the truck with Chet."

He walked to the next vehicle where Charley was held under the guns of half a dozen of el-Abri's guerrillas. L'Heureux was tied hand and foot in a sitting position on one of the benches under the truck canvas. The sergeant in charge of the guard would not allow Durell to get too near the prisoner.

"He is a coward, this one," the guard said quietly. "He shakes and sweats with fear."

Durell nodded. "Charley?"

"Durell, get me out of this," L'Heureux whispered from the darkness in the truck. "He's going to kill me when he gets back."

151

"It will only be what you asked for."

"For God's sake, Durell—!"

"You knew the risks you were taking," Durell said.

"Look, I'm an American, you can't let these gooks do anything they want with me! I got a right to a fair trial, don't I? Look, I'll tell you and the French authorities everything you want to know. You've got the money back, right? What you want is the names of the Frenchmen who organized this deal to make propaganda and get a grip on the Paris government through it, right?"

"Do you know their names?"

"Sure, I know who they are."

"Do you have proof?"

"I've got proof," L'Heureux said eagerly. His big frame looked crushed, sunken in on itself. His face was haggard in the shadows within the truck. "I've got letters they wrote, some of their operational plans. They've got some big men in the French Parliament, in the Army, big businessmen in Paris and Algiers, too. They want the war to go on until they get a good grip on the government, see, and run things their way."

"Where are these documents?"

L'Heureux hesitated. "Can you help me?"

"Where are they?"

"You've got to get me out of this first."

"I can't promise anything," Durell said. "And I won't make any bargains with you."

L'Heureux said desperately, "But it's all I got left to make you help me."

"You don't have anything left, Charley. Not even your life."

"How can I trust you, then?" he whispered.

Durell started to walk away. One of the guards laughed.

"Durell, wait!"

Durell turned, but he did not go back to the truck.

"Look, I gave the documents, all of them, to Madeleine," L'Heureux said quickly. "She kept them in her apartment in Paris. We hid them behind a painting, some picture of the Seine, in her living room. They're still there."

"All right," Durell said.

"What are you going to do now?" L'Heureux asked, after a pause.

"I'm not sure what I can do," Durell said.

152

He turned and walked into the garden of el-Abri's house.

He found the Kabyle in the walled area behind the *mechta*. It was quiet here, secure from the whining wind that blew sand and the smell of death throughout the village. The old olive tree stood like a twisted skeleton against the starlit sky. Durell did not see el-Abri at once. He looked first at the tree, and saw that the mutilated bodies of the old people had been cut down. Then he saw their mute forms on the flower beds under the tree, beneath a blanket. He didn't see el-Abri until he turned toward the house, and then he saw the Kabyle standing in the doorway with a knife in his hand.

"Old friend, listen to me," Durell said.

"Stay where you are. Do not come near me."

"I ask you to think twice of what you're going to do."

"Do not ask me anything. Do not speak to me now."

"I will," Durell said. "I've got to." He drew a deep breath. He knew that what he was going to say meant success or failure, perhaps life or death. He could not remember a time when so much had depended on the words he chose and the care with which he spoke them. El-Abri was almost deranged with grief. His anger was as wide in sweep and cruelty as the desert that had bred him. He looked like a stranger to Durell, a man he did not know any more.

"Listen to me," he said gently. "You said yourself that they were innocent, these old people."

"Be quiet, Durell. I warn you."

"It would be wrong to hold my tongue now. You believe in an eye for an eye, in vengeance, one death to avenge other deaths. But when does this end, Hadji, and what will be gained?"

The Kabyle turned his head slowly. His eyes flashed white. "You would have me spare L'Heureux?"

"Yes. Give him back to me."

"How can you ask that now, after what my eyes have seen here in this house of peace?"

"There are thousands of houses in this land where peace once lived, but they are peaceful no more. Like your house, death and grief has come to stay forever. You are not alone."

"You ask too much!" el-Abri suddenly shouted.

"I ask only for reason and justice."

There was silence. Then the Arab said quietly, "Those

are the words Orrin Boston used, when he first persuaded me to surrender."

"Were those words wrong?"

"You ask me to think of words now?"

"I ask you to think of what you gain and what you lose by killing L'Heureux now, in the heat of your anger, in the ice of your grief."

"You talk too much, Durell. You weigh our friendship with words that mean nothing. You think I cannot kill you, too, if you anger me?"

"I am not your enemy. And L'Heureux is only the little finger of one hand of the enemy who killed your parents."

"What are you saying?"

"Chop off a finger, and does your enemy die? Killing L'Heureux will end nothing. Think about it, and you will see it is the truth. But if you keep him alive, like a fatal poison, you will kill them. Keep him alive and talking, to poison them. He has already talked to me. Alive, L'Heureux is your weapon of vengeance. Kill him, and you do only what your enemies would want you to do, what they would do themselves if they had him."

The Kabyle came out of the doorway and crossed the garden. His tall, thin figure moved stiffly and mechanically. He kept the knife in his hand. He stood before Durell and his face in the starlight was a face of stone, ravaged by wind and sand. He put the knife at Durell's throat. Durell did not step back. He felt the sharp pricking of the point as it cut into his skin.

"My way is clear. Do not confuse me!"

"I will talk until you cut my throat," Durell said.

The pressure of the knife increased momentarily. Durell felt a thin, warm trickle of blood run down his neck. He stood still. He heard the ragged breathing of the Kabyle. El-Abri's eyes glistened unnaturally in the dim light.

"I swore to my dead father and mother—"

"You swore vengeance. But L'Heureux did not kill them."

"He was one of those who did."

"Only a small man, a tool, an agent of others."

El-Abri hesitated. "That much I know to be true."

"There is more truth in the rest of what I will say."

The Kabyle trembled. "You are a brave man, Durell."

"It is only that I know I am right."

154

The knife was taken away from his throat.

Durell did not dare let his relief show in any relaxation of his face, his body, or his voice.

"Sit down," he said. "There is time yet. Once you were willing to surrender to the French because you found yourself out of sympathy with certain factions who seemed to be gaining control of the Algerian independence movement. You disapproved of their terror methods, of their implacable refusal to negotiate and compromise. You thought it was wrong for the extremists to murder Moslem Algerians here and in France simply because they saw some reason in the French side, too. Now their terror has visited you personally, giving you a grievous loss. You see with your own eyes what this war has done, turning men into savages, killing the innocent, bathing the land in senseless blood."

"The French have been equally guilty," el-Abri said.

"There is still a majority of Frenchmen who seek a reasonable solution. All it requires is for passion to be controlled and rightful claims to be weighed in justice. No problem is beyond solution by compromise and calm judgment. You saw that once, when you were willing to surrender. You see it now."

"No."

"Baroumi can be made into a trap for those who push this war to excess for their own selfish ends. There are men who are greedy for power on both sides. In either case, be it one kind of dictatorship or another, your people will lose, and the entire free world will lose."

"What can one do?" the Kabyle said quietly. He had stopped trembling. He put the knife away. "You offer no solution."

"You can lay down your arms on honorable terms, as Orrin Boston suggested. You agreed once, and you were betrayed by L'Heureux. But you can turn L'Heureux over to the proper authorities. If you torture and kill him, you accomplish only what your enemies wish—to stop his mouth and wipe him from the earth. But if he names the names of our true enemies—yours and mine, Hadji—and lives to charge them with his own tongue, then the most good will be accomplished. I want to expose the cunning, greedy men on both sides who fatten on violence and terror, wherever it is. You and I are not enemies. We fight for the same ends. For peace, for the right of a man to walk the world in secure dignity."

"And if these men are exposed by what L'Heureux knows?"

"You said yourself that it may only be a straw. A small thing, perhaps. But can we say which straw will tip the scales toward a better world?"

El-Abri walked to the olive tree near the garden wall and looked down at the two bodies under the blanket by the flower bed. He stood with his back to Durell for a long time. The village was silent. There was only the endless wind in the upper fronds of the date palms nearby. Durell said nothing more. He waited.

El-Abri spoke in a strangled voice. "No."

He turned and walked to the garden gate. His figure was tall and stiff. He carried himself strangely in his angry grief. "Your talk is not for me, Durell. The burdens of the world are not my world. My people are dead and I have in my hands the man who helped to kill them."

"Your people are dead and the burden is yours," Durell said. "If you refuse it, you are also responsible, and they died for nothing."

El-Abri was at the gate. Durell felt the exhaustion of defeat move over him like a great, engulfing wave. He looked down at his wounded hand. It was bleeding again, and the pain was severe. He watched a drop of his blood fall upon the dry soil of the garden. It didn't matter. He had fought many battles. If he lost this one, it would not bring the world down in crashing flames.

El-Abri halted. His tall figure seemed to sway. He took the knife and held it in both hands, looking at it. The starlight winked on the cold steel blade.

He turned to Durell. Durell waited.

Suddenly the Kabyle drove the knife against the stone garden wall. The blade shattered and broke with a high, clear, ringing sound. The point fell to the earth. El-Abri dropped the hilt after it and turned back to Durell.

"You can have your prisoner. And you can take me and my men with you."

Chapter Twenty-one

ALGIERS sparkled in the evening sun like a handful of jewels dropped by a careless giant between the sea and the Sahel Hills. It did not look like a city at war. The Rue

Michelet was crowded, the narrow streets were clogged with noisy traffic of Renaults and motorbikes; the terraced stairways angling between the villas that hung between sea and sky were thronged with people hurrying home from work or shopping. The only evidence of war was in a roll of barbed wire guarding a bank entrance near the terrace café where Durell sat, and the colorful uniforms and green berets of the French elite paratroopers.

He was waiting for Monsieur Brumont, due from Paris. He had checked into the St. George shortly after noon, consulted with various officials in the sprawling complex of the Governor-General's building. The surrender of el-Abri, the recovery of a quarter of a million American dollars in rebel territory, and the capture of Charles L'Heureux had combined to send officers and politicians there into a state of excitement that had kept the wires to Paris sizzling hot.

Tomorrow the first news release would break, but Durell was not concerned with that now. He felt a bone-weary exhaustion that had led him back to the St. George after a doctor had attended to his injured hand. He had had a long hot bath, then dinner, then a two-hour nap shot through with gray nightmares.

The evening was warm in Algiers. He sipped an *apéritif* in the sidewalk café near the hotel and waited for Brumont. People chattered all around him, read newspapers, talked, flirted, laughed, and watched the passers-by.

He felt lonelier than he had ever felt in his life.

He was watching for Brumont's taxi from the Maison Blanche airport when he saw Jane Larkin get out of a cab and walk quickly across the broad mosaic sidewalk toward the hotel.

Durell stood up and she saw him and came his way. She looked different. She had found new clothing, and she wore a pencil-slim dress that only accented the firm lines of her body. Her blond hair had been washed and combed and she looked as if nothing had happened, until he saw her eyes. He pulled out a chair for her and she joined him at his table.

"I can only stay a moment," she said. She sounded breathless. "I have to get back to the hospital as soon as possible."

"How is Chet?"

"He'll be all right now. They've got the bullet out. The

157

rest of it is just a lot of bruises. I'm so grateful to you, Durell."

"How long will you stay in Algiers?" he asked.

"I don't know," Jane said. "It depends on Chet."

"I thought you were so anxious to get back to Texas."

"Yesterday I thought I was anxious to have a lot of things." The waiter came with a Pernod at Durell's signal, and she twisted the glass in her fingers. She looked up at Durell, and he thought her eyes looked very different. Her mouth was no longer petulant when she smiled. "Yesterday I was someone else, I'm afraid. Someone not very nice at all."

"What is Chet going to do?"

"He's planning to renew his contract with the oil exploration company. There's a lot of work to do here. If they can find oil in the Sahara, it may change a great many things in Algeria."

"I see."

Jane said quietly, "Anyway, I told Chet about the baby."

"I didn't know about that," Durell said. "Congratulations."

"I was horrible to him. I wasn't going to tell him at all. Not until after we got home." She flushed and lifted her Pernod and set it down again without tasting it. "This sounds like a confession, I suppose, but I've learned so much in the last day or two that I still haven't digested it all. There's one thing, however. I'm going to stay with Chet, no matter what he decides to do."

"I'm glad," Durell said.

She laughed. "You should see Chet. I have a lot to make up for." She picked up her purse and stood. Her eyes were bright. She looked happy for the first time since Durell had met her, and he felt a touch of envy and wondered about it. "You must excuse me now. I have to hurry and get back to the hospital."

He stood up with her and shook hands. "Of course. Good luck, Jane."

"Thank you. Goodbye."

He watched her hurry into the hotel and when he turned back to his drink, the world seemed emptier for him.

M. Brumont was wearing the same purplish blue suit with the wide, pointed lapels that Durell had seen him

158

wear in Paris. And the same ubiquitous black felt hat and raincoat, although Algiers sparkled in the warmth of the evening sun.

"I have just come from the Governor-General's," Brumont said, after they shook hands and he ordered brandy. "Everyone there is in quite a flap. I had quite a time getting those idiots to release L'Heureux into the custody of my two men for shipment to Paris."

"What are you going to do with him?" Durell asked.

"He will be questioned by my colleagues at Paris Intelligence and the Deuxième Bureau, naturally." Brumont looked fat and harried, his black moustache bristling with excitement. "We followed the directions you gave us in your wire, you know, and searched Sardelle's apartment in Paris. We found L'Heureux' documents. Political dynamite, m'sieu. Proof of a definite conspiracy to prolong the war until the people of France are desperate for any peace, regardless of justice. Heads will roll in Parliament, I assure you. And here in Algiers, as well. It will be of vast effect in helping to bring about a reasonable solution to this distressing matter."

"Have you been in touch with my Embassy?" Durell asked.

"They expect you in Paris tomorrow. Arrangements are being made in regard to the disposition of L'Heureux. There will be no difficulty on that, since for once—" Brumont's smile was wry—"For once, your State Department sees eye to eye with us in this matter."

"That's something, anyway," Durell said.

"You sound sad, m'sieu."

"I suppose I'm simply tired."

"In any case, permit me to offer my personal congratulations. You have performed a valuable service for us. It is my hope that France will be the better for what you have done, whatever the agony in political circles. It may even hasten the end of the war here."

Brumont stood up and they shook hands again. The fat little Frenchman consulted a huge gold pocket watch. "I am due back at the Governor-General's office. L'Heureux will be flown to Paris on the midnight plane, and I will return with him. You would not wish to come back with us?"

"Tomorrow will be time enough."

Brumont smiled and winked. He looked like a cherub gone to seed. "I understand. One evening in Algiers is

159

almost the same as Paris—especially when one has a rendezvous, eh?"

"I have no rendezvous, unfortunately," Durell said.

"But Mlle. Padgett—your lovely friend that you left in Paris—you have not seen her yet?"

"She's back in Washington by now," Durell said.

"You are mistaken, m'sieu. She is here in Algiers. She remained over in Paris and begged me to take her when I came here this afternoon. Surely you have seen her by now? I was wondering, if you will pardon the curiosity, why you sat here so much alone, a man like you—"

Durell was on his feet. "Where is she?"

Brumont smiled and winked again. "Perhaps in your room, m'sieu. Where else?" He sighed. "And now I will not keep you, since I have much work to do. Adieu, m'sieu."

"Goodbye," Durell said again.

When Brumont had hailed a taxi, Durell turned and walked quickly along the broad sidewalk to his hotel. Evening had come, but a pale violet light still lingered over the Mediterranean and the Sahel Hills. Lights twinkled and shone all over the city. He got out of the elevator and moved with a long stride down the corridor, and all at once it seemed as if he were back in the dream again, with all the closed doors barring understanding around him. He walked faster. His door was at the end of the hall. It was closed. But then he saw a thin line of light shining under it and he knew someone was there.

Deirdre opened the door before he reached it.

"Surprise, darling," she said.

And she said, "Welcome home, Sam."

She stood back as he halted. She was beautiful. She looked scrubbed and rosy, as if she had just stepped from his shower, and he saw she had invaded his suitcase and taken out his bathrobe. It was wrapped loosely around her body. She looked inviting and desirable.

Durell moved quickly through the open door toward her.

68-7-5